This is a work of fiction. Similarities to real people, places, or events are entirely coincidental.

RUNNING THE TRAIN AND ALL THE STORIES: THE COMPLETE BEN MILES COLLECTION

RUNNNG THE TRAIN...

AND ALL THE STORIES

THE ULTIMATE BEN MILES Mystery Collection

By Costa Koutsoutis

for chontel, for mom and dad, for papou and yiayia and papou and yiayia, for john, for g, for everyone who ever believed in me

Table of Contents

Coffee & Sandwiches (Flotsam & Frontmatter)

The Original Crew

Late Arrivals

The End of the Day (Jetsam & Backmatter)

INTRODUCTION

I always wanted to be a writer.

I know everyone always says that, but it's true. I remember filling notebooks with diary entries, stories, character descriptions, terrible doodles and sketches of comic book and movie superhero characters I'd invented. In college I spent almost a year worldbuilding and writing my first serious forays into fiction, really awful stuff in hindsight. It's lost to the world, in the ether of an anonymous online writing group/serialized subscription service. Good thing too, because it was mostly an amalgamation of everything I was consuming at the time with no filter.

Ben Miles is, ironically enough, one of those types of creations, a filterless spawn from my unadulterated love of mystery, crime, detectives, and espionage. Before comic books, alternative literature, or anything, there were paperbacks, pulpy *Indiana Jones* adaptations, John Sanford's "Lucas Davenport" stories, Kinky Friedman, and the works of William Heffernan, who I was obsessed with as a teen.

Anyway, I hope you like this collection of stories. I write this in transition at a kitchen table with plans for a move in the works. Writing keeps me sane, but also keeps me from packing funny enough, I'd rather be here hammering away like a caveman with a rock making a new tool.

My parents always encouraged me to read, and I consider that the greatest gift I've ever gotten. This is dedicated to them.

costa/columbus oh/july 2012

PREFACE

It's been a long time since I was here with Ben Miles, an even longer time since that hot summer I had nothing going on, no job, a bad relationship, and for a week...no power, leaving me camped out in the local coffeeshop nursing a single iced coffee to justify being plugged in all day to charge my phone and run my computer. So why not sit and write a novella and a collection of short stories about a bounty hunter and private eye?

That summer was a moment that I don't think I could ever duplicate. I was writing a lot, but mostly because I was unhappy honestly and escaping into reading and writing, I was broke and poor and already thinking about some level of escape plan to regroup. But I had this gulf of time that needed to be filled, and the way this poured out of me so naturally made me suddenly recognize that if I stopped fighting with myself about telling stories that I thought people wanted to hear, the stories I wanted to tell were so much easier to do.

It's been a while since then for me, and maybe a little for Ben Miles too. He never got anywhere, but he was the first character I ever really created fully-formed in my mind that came out so easily, lanky and loose and confident at the wrong times, unsure at the times he needed to be more assertive, kind of floating around life and content to not have to figure it out or have existential angst or dread, so he's always had a soft spot in my brain and heart. I figured

I might as well try to give him a better home than my first attempt all that time ago.

Now, I sit in my own home instead of a coffee shop working on this, with a little bit more knowledge and a lot more callouses when it comes to writing and to how to properly format, edit, put stories together, that sort of thing. I've even managed a bit of critical and nonfiction thinking about these types of stories and mysteries, where the object or the perpetrator isn't quite as important as the mood, and that mood often means a lot to the reading experience.

Anyway, most of what's been put in this new edition was here at first, but there' a bit more added now, some stuff is fixed, and it's now got a few tidbits I found featuring the work of New York's worst bail bondsman-slash-private eye who has far-more skilled friends.

costa/new york ny/may 2020

The Original Crew

"Mob."

DON'T LOOK.

Don't look, don't look, don't look. That's the first rule, and the only rule that he could remember. Tailing someone is a weird science full of arcane rules built up over years of Ivy-League spies, cops, and shield-wielding detectives losing monumentally and being ten years' worth of experience behind cons, PI's, and any kid worth his salt who's ever walked to and from school.

Ben focused on the hot dog he was eating, hot and slathered in everything, dripping onions onto his hand, eating as he walked. He almost tripped on his own feet sucking the onions off his wrist, not paying attention to tall, white, balding, two hundred pounds, in khakis and a green button-up shirt twenty feet ahead. Erratic through the mid-lunch crowd in midtown Manhattan, crossing the street with extra care to check that his briefcase was in his arms, wrapped up in a khaki coat matching his pants, a weird bundle that was attracting more attention that it deflected.

Still, the mark was paranoid enough to keep looking backwards, at one point even having stopped suddenly, Ben bumping into him, "Sorry" floating from the PI's lips as he floated on by, ducking into a storefront to let the other man pass him on the street before exiting what turned out to be a sex shop, down in the Village where he'd first started following the man, walking the whole way. At this point he didn't even know what he was looking for, fumbling for the smartphone in his pocket as he finished the last of the hot dog, the balding man, sweat stains growing through his shirt, now walking faster, noticeably trying to get somewhere.

Change of pace. The means two things, either he knows that he's being followed and is an amateur about it, or something is about to happen and he's showing, giving away massive physical tells. He hadn't looked backwards in a while, and Ben broke the first rule, looking hard at him from behind, moving with purpose now to follow him through the tail-end of a lunch crowd. This was even stupider, giving yourself away in an ever-thinning and ever-disappearing cover of crowd, making your obvious movement the worst kind of giveaway.

And then he's gone. A turn and all of a sudden, the mark is gone, not there, and Ben's obviously giving himself away, standing still on the sidewalk and looking around frantically. And then there, across the street, coming the opposite direction.

Tall, white, balding, with a rumpled khaki suit jacket covering his green button-up shirt, two hundred pounds, matching khaki pants, walking smoothly, confident.

His hands empty.

Dialing from memory, Ben held the phone up. "Come on, come on, pick up," he said into the dial tone, hearing one, two, three, four, five ringtones, nothing picking up. "Shit." His client, the voice at the other end of the phone line with a name he can't remember and an assurance of payment that a ping on the laptop told him meant that there was a deposit in his bank account, wasn't picking up. Clients always pick up when you call. Always. They won't pick up when their mothers call, but the PI? Always.

Shit. Shit shit shit fucking shit, holy shit what the hell is goin...

The explosion's noise was huge, though the puff of smoke sending glittery paper and white shreds of fabric into the air wasn't as massive as the noise warranted. Compressed air probably, forcing the confetti into the drafts between the tall buildings as somewhere, a hi-fi stereo in a car started to play and the crowd froze for a second before moving, key people dancing in time and in rhythm and the flash mob screamed in unison and danced to themselves, glitter and white scraps floating back down.

A police siren was wailing close, as cops swarmed the intersection, the music already dying down as people scattered, shed coats, melding into the gathered crowd of laughing and gawking onlookers, a few had joined into the dancing, just out of time with the screams and steps to make the movement seem actually spontaneous instead of what Ben was realizing was more than him being played, an elaborate art project prank. Somewhere, video rolled for YouTube or whatever.

A single scrap of the glittery paper was on Ben's shoe, and he leaned down, plucked it off the ground to look at the cheap reflective surface, scissor-sliced reflective shiny Christmas wrapping in small rectangles. He turned over the scrap, and there it was, written in what looked like precise handwritten letters, all lower-case but probably computer-printed.

Fooled you.

"Old Dogs"

"LOOK, JUST ASK HIM."

"I am not going to ask him anything."

"Come on, ask him! It'll take you ten minutes, and then you can leave and not have to deal with me…"

"For another six months until you need something again, and refuse to stop leaving me messages demanding that I help you out of some hole you've gotten yourself into!"

"So, you'll ask him?"

"Ben, I am telling you that you're wrong, it's not him!"

Ben stared at her as they sat in the tiny, dimly-lit café. Outside the trains rattled overhead on the elevated tracks, and the foot traffic and cars was a constant din. Despite the loud hum of the industrial air conditioner and the large-scale Venetian blinds lowered over the front windows and glass door, the hot hair and bright sun was fighting to filter into the small tile-lined front room. Faded and peeling old maps of Greece and photos of men in moustaches lined the walls, some in frames of stained old silver, some in battered cheap wood. Fake Greco-Romanesque columns were in the corners, with fake ivy twined around them. Mismatched chairs sat around metal tables scattered around the café, which was empty save for one grouping around the table furthest back from the door and front windows.

Three old men, consumed in their card game and keeping score on a battered old legal pad, were yelling at each other periodically in Greek, peppered occasionally with heavily-accented English that was probably just their own takes on English slurs. They seemed to be ignoring Ben and Kalli, who were at the table next to them. No one else seemed to be in the coffee shop in the middle of Astoria.

Ben Miles, a PI and sometimes-bondsman, rubbed his face with his hands, elbows on the cheap peeling linoleum of the table. Late-twenties, scruffy, and looking every bit the constant mess. "Look, I'm telling you, he's the guy."

"How do you know?" Kalli, mid- to late-thirties, put together, a more successful PI and bondswoman, the kind with a real office and employees, looked at him suspiciously, drinking from her glass of water that a reluctant waiter had brought them when the two had walked in and sat down. They hadn't seen him since. "I know you think you're this great 'finder' or whatever, but I am telling you that you're wrong. That's Grigories Kafilas, the owner of the DVD Emporium. Every Greek kid in the borough knows who he is, we always went to him for movies, even back when it was all VHS. He's the bootleg movie king of Queens."

Ben pulled a battered and much-folded piece of paper, a computer printout of a photo, from his pants pocket, smoothing the crinkled image out on the table. "Look," he said in a stage whisper, "He's got the scar on the back of his hand, where the tattoo would have been. He's the same age, the same height, same eye color..."

Kalli put her hand on his arm. "Ben, do you know how many old Greek men are in this neighborhood? With dark brown eyes and scarred hands? This guy?" She frowned, reading the scrawled marker writing on the paper, "Frank Kroger? He's not even Greek!"

Ben leaned back in his chair, frowning. "I know I'm right," he said, re-folding the picture and putting it back in his pocket. "Fred Kroger's a German-Italian kid from Ohio who works as a clean-up guy for what ends up becoming the Cleveland Mafia in the seventies. He disappears with his boss's ledgers one day, mails the ledgers to the FBI in Washington, DC, from what the Feds eventually discover was a post office in Iowa.

"Then, Kafilas shows up in New York the same time Kroger disappears, looks the same, has a scarred hand where a tattoo's been? The same place that Kroger was known to have a tattoo? Ends up owning a video rental store and then a DVD place? Everyone I've talked to has told me Kroger was obsessed with movies, always wanted to own a theater or something, spent every spare minute he had going to the movies.

"I've been following this guy around Astoria for almost a week, and he's slipped up almost a few times, when he thinks that no one is watching, in the way he carries himself, the way he walks. Kalli, it's him. I can feel it, it's a gut thing."

"That's your proof?" Kalli shook her head, clearly confused. "That's the silliest story I've ever heard from you. Look, I've always been willing to help you, you know that. And I've almost always believed you when you came to these ridiculous conclusions because they usually turn out to be true, but this is too much. This is my old neighborhood, these are my people. I'm pretty sure I've even been in this place before with my dad!" Kalli pulled an iPhone out of her inner coat pocket, thumbing through the screen. "Look, you can't just ask me to go around, talking to these old men like that. I have connections here I need to maintain, unlike you."

Ben stood up from the table. "Okay, fine. You don't believe me, you don't wanna do me this one little favor. Then I'll ask him." He moved around the small table to walk over to the group of old men, and paused.

The group of three were gone, their game apparently long-over. The old man Kalli had called Kafilas was standing there, leaning slightly on one of the chairs, watching the two argue. Ben could see the remains of the sheet of paper and pencil used to keep score tucked into his shirt pocket, next to what looked like a pair of folded glasses, big old-man glasses.

"You should take more risks and listen to him, young miss," he said, with no trace of any Greek, his Midwestern accent barely noticeable, "Whose are you?"

"Y-Yianni...Yianni Kiliaris' granddaughter," Kalli said, in shock. "I'm his daughter's daughter."

"Good family," the old man said. "So," he moved to sit at their table, with Kalli scrambling to pull a chair back for him almost deferentially as Ben grinned ear-to-ear, stood there. The old man sat down and reached into his shirt pocket, pulling out a pair of thick-lensed glasses, perching them on his face before looking back up. "You are, young man?"

"Your brother's grandsons hired me to find you, Mr. Kroger," Ben said, "they'd heard about you and the story of how you crossed the

Novelli family back in Ohio. Wanted to know what happened to you, so they called someone who called someone who called me. I, ah...I find stuff."

"Stuff?" Kroger said, looking at him over his glasses.

"Well, people too," Ben said, shuffling through his pockets. "I swear, it's a real job, I'm not a weirdo."

"Ben is a private investigator," Kalli said, "and despite the stupid look on his face, not a bad one."

"An investigator, really?" Kroger said, "What, like a PI? A gumshoe, a detective?" He turned to look at Kalli, "and you? Are you his girl Friday? Have you seen *The Thin Man*? One of my favorite films. How about *The Long Goodbye*?" He laughed to himself. "Well, at least you don't work for the Novellis. Wouldn't be the first to get close, but I haven't seen any of them in a long time. One time, one of them came here, asking about me, asking if any old Italian men lived in the neighborhood. I near about pissed my pants, sitting right over there." He pointed to the corner table he'd been at earlier, playing cards. "I know that not everyone has been fooled in the neighborhood, and a few know something about me is off..."

"The Novelli family's long-gone, Mr. Kroger," Ben said, before the old man cut him off. "Please, call me Grigories. I've answered to that name longer than Frank Kroger."

"Mr. Kafilas, sorry. The Novelli family's long gone, the FBI took them apart like a fat kid eating a chicken wing years ago. Salvadore Novelli died in prison, I talked to Frankie Rolo's son, Ronnie? He ended up in the ATF funny enough, but he said that his dad's friends all died off before anyone could really pass on anything about you to the newer generation of guys, so you've pretty much been forgotten as far as they're concerned. At least, that's what it looks like to me."

The old man didn't say anything, his hands on the tabletop. Ben could see the tops of his hands, gnarled and worn, the scar on the back of his left hand still obvious. "I took a strip of sandpaper to it when I got on the train to New York. Took me an hour and I bled all over, I had to rip up a shirt to cover it up. I was so stupid, I probably could have just waited and it'd have faded away. I ended up working at the docks, was in the sun all day, messed up my hands a bunch of times, would've hid it.

"Everyone you talked to is right, you know. I loved the movies, always took girls there, even went alone. There is something about being in the dark and seeing another world and a story that is not your own, it felt freeing. I guess I should have opened up a restaurant, maybe then you would've never found me. But I have always loved the movies. Maybe if I'd been born now, and was young like you, I'd have made my own movies, become famous, made other people feel the way that I felt when I watched them. But back then?"

He sighed. "I was never going to get made by the family, because my father was a German. What else could I do? It was impossible for a son of an Italian widow in Cleveland to do anything except work for the Novelli family, you know. But in the end, it was too much, seeing what they did and what I did. So I did what I did. You would be surprised at how easily I got the books, back then security was something none of us thought about. Even now, my stores, just locking the doors and putting the alarm on, no one thought of that. Who would dare cross the Novellis?"

The old ex-gangster-turned-DVD-mogul stood up suddenly, ambling over to the counter of the empty café, his hands in his pockets. "My brother had already left for the army and was in Europe at the time, on his way to becoming an officer. He died in a training accident a few months later. My mother was dead, lung cancer from working in the factories all those years. I didn't have anything holding me back.

"I stopped and changed trains at one point on my way to New York, and mailed the books to the F.B.I from an address I found in the yellow pages. Did you know that? The Federal Bureau of Investigation used to be listed in the phone book!" He laughed. "I thought I was so clever, pretending to be a Greek. It wasn't easy, but I knew enough of the language, we'd had a few work for us in Cleveland. The Italians, they treated them like shit..." he trailed off suddenly, and turned around. "So, what now? You and me, we road trip like a movie back to Ohio? Are we happily reunited?"

Kalli stood up from the table, and walked towards the door, pausing before she stepped out into the busy and bright-hot street. Ben walked over to the table the old men had been playing cards at, ripping a piece of paper from the legal pad and grabbing the pencil. He sat back down with the old former gangster, and scrawled something down. "This is my number. You call me if you need anything at all."

"Alright," Kafilas said. "And this other number?"

Ben stood up. "His name is Michael, he's your oldest grand-nephew. He and his wife would love to meet you. They live in Cincinnati. He married a Greek woman, actually."

He walked towards the door, following after Kalli. "Give him a call sometime, he's a nice guy. They really would like to meet you." He opened the door to the café, the sounds of the crowds and the street spilling in along with a burst of hot air, and slipped out.

"Fireflies"

THE SUMMER EVENING was still light, seven PM and the sun still up, the kind of evenings when college kids would sit on the patios of bars and talk deep thoughts, kids would run around outside marveling that they could play and ride bikes after five PM.

He sat on the back steps, the .38 revolver in his hands pointing down, staring off into space. Even though it was light out, the fireflies were starting to blip in and out, and a post-rainstorm wind made the air cool enough for a long-sleeved shirt.

The gun belonged to an ex-cop, a friend of a friend who used to use it as a backup piece. A throwaway picked up somewhere, it had had so many owners before, it probably hadn't even originally been sold in New York State. The cop ended up retiring, and $100 and a good bottle of whiskey got Ben the gun to have around, just in case.

The six chambers were always loaded, had always been loaded since Ben got it, and there was an unopened box of ammunition under the bed of his loft, but Ben had never used it, not even for target shooting, once in the three years he'd owned it, wrapped in an old heavy metal band t-shirt in the guitar case under the bed next to the emergency kit and box of ammunition. Guns were terrible inventions, stupid tools used by stupid people.

Then the call had come.

"Yeah, Ben Miles here, PI and bail bonds."

"Hey man, what's up Ben? It's Rick."

Ben had hung up the cellphone, turned it and his personal cellphone off, and then checked out the windows of his third-story walkup loft. No one was on the street. He grabbed the bag of cash and some clothes he kept under the bed, the gun, the box of ammo, threw it all in a large knockoff military duffel he'd gotten from a Chinese street fair a year ago, scribbled a quick note, left it by the door, and left.

That had been a week ago. He was in New Jersey at a friend's house, "house-sitting" near Montclair. He'd spent the past three nights at bars near the college campus, drinking cold weak Bud and watching New Jersey high school baseball with the sound too low, college girls in too-short shorts saddling up to the bar to giggle and order Long Island Iced Teas, watching him out of the corners of their eyes poorly, deciding whether or not he was better or worse than clean-cut and significantly-louder college boys.

So maybe it hadn't been that bad.

The house phone had rung yesterday night, and he'd let it ring a few times before answering. "Yeah."

"Hey Ben, I'll be by tomorrow, see you then."

Rick was a former bail bondsman who did a stretch for B-and-E thanks to Ben. Rick had a nasty reputation of shaking down his clients for cash stashes and dope during "home checks." He and Ben knew each other vaguely, the way most PI's and bail bond types did, but Ben crossed him when working a case a few years ago. A few calls had the cops catching the big man who wore

MMA brand-name shirts a size too tight in a strange house with no warrant, a bag of a bank's cash, and an unregistered Glock with the serial number filed off. It got him what he deserved, but even better it kept him out of Ben's hair while combing upstate New York for a missing kid, a kid that Rick wanted too and considered his big "score," help him get into the news, book deals, a reality TV series.

Rick was the worst kind of bondsman, the kind who wore a gun and a useless custom "Bounty Hunter USA" star badge on his belt like a cowboy, thought he was some sort of comic book anti-hero. Kalli Kiliaris, Ben's actual-professional PI friend and occasional boss/contact, hated the man, muttered all sorts of Greek obscenities about him whenever his name came up about his ability to read, his sexual proclivities, and his general animal-brute brain.

But he'd been good, in a way. Still was good, apparently, good enough to find Ben a state over when he was probably fresh out of jail and all his old work contacts cutting him off before he could even say hi as he'd call them collect from a payphone.

The fireflies were getting brighter now, and the low din of kids playing on the streets like they tended to do during the summer, especially after a thunderstorm, was starting to die down as parents called them in for dinner, bedtimes, summer school homework. Ben could hear the gate that led around the house open and close, and Rick came up the side, into the backyard.

His hands were in his pants pockets, his clothes, a set of faded Dickies and white t-shirt, stiff with prison starch, probably donated from some church basement clothing drive for poor souls just trying to rehabilitate themselves. He had a shoddy cheap kid's backpack slung across one shoulder, the plastic fabric fraying and the strap straining, tied with duct tape at one part. Rick was a big man, and probably had thought of prison as some sort of trial-by-fire experience. It showed, he hadn't let himself go to fat or anything, with a big fat barrel chest and big arms, shitty prison tattoos on one arm.

Jesus Christ, really? Ben thought, still not moving or saying anything, just staring, the gun still in his hand.

"Hey, Ben."

"Hi Rick."

"You got a permit for that?" Rick nudged his chin at the .38, and he grinned. "Do you even know how to shoot?"

"Your parole officer knows you're in New Jersey? He know you left your sister's basement in the Bronx?"

"Come on, man, what the state of New York don't know can't hurt them." That had been how Rick had worked when Ben first heard of him, then seen him in action when they first met in person. Trying to smooth-talk, get you comfortable, not expect the 250-lbs. shot to the solar plexus for "resisting." Resisting, like he's a real cop, Ben remembered thinking the first time he saw the man in action.

Ben didn't move still, sitting on the steps, letting his trigger finger hand loose. Even when the big man knelt down, try to seem like he wasn't a threat, just a fellow bondsman sitting down to rap and get down to business, and Ben knew he was sizing up the gun. Rick was a lunk, but not a complete idiot, with a stretch in some PMC in the first Gulf War, knew a functional gun when he saw one versus a shitty piece that barely could fire used just for show. "Look, I know you did what you had to do, and I respect that. Hell, if anything you did me a favor getting me tossed in the clink like th..."

Ben suddenly jumped, tackling Rick and holding the revolver in his fist like a rock, a club, punching it into the other man on the side of the head. They tumbled back into the grass of the yard and Rick, white as a baby's ass, prison-strong from five years with nothing to do but fight black gangbangers and lift weights, punched once, twice, three times into Ben's sides, looking for and finding his kidneys. That was stupid, so fucking stupid, so goddamn fucking stupid Ben thought as the pain blossomed in his sides like a dozen needles, trying to hit the other man again with the gun like a club while not gasping too hard in pain.

They were struggling for the gun, Rick's hands on Ben's trying to pry his fingers from the grip, the shattered butt falling to bits after being used to smack Rick in the side of the head, and Ben could feel Rick pry one, two, three, four fingers off the gun, the trigger tightening, aiming somewhere in between the two of them, clicking once, twice, nothing. Ben smashed hard as he could awkwardly backhand into the already-bleeding side of Rick's head, trying desperately to get the upper hand. *I am so fucked, so colossally fucked.*

The ex-con was on top now, one fist cocked back to probably crush Ben's eye socket, blood trickling down his ear from the first hit with the metal pistol. That dumb-brute look, animal rage that Ben knew Rick hated people to see and realize how fucking stupid he was in

the end, was in his eyes, the look that said I Am Going To Fuck You
Up.

"Alright, that's enough," a voice said from the back door, Wesley
Willows. Fifty-ish, Rick's parole officer, old-school, standing there
leaning against the doorframe. The big black stick in his hands
looked like an old-fashioned police baton, or even some sort of
weirdo freak sex toy, if not for the metal prongs at one end. There
was no way in hell a PO would have a shock prod like that
normally, not on the books, but Rick was big and a brute and
Willows knew the only way you put brutes down was the way
you put down a bull. Over his shoulder, an actual cop stood, a
kid practically, clearly wanting to intercede, maybe even shoot
something, but unsure of how to enforce any real authority against
the violence.

Rick knew the drill, letting his balled fist relax, getting up, arms
out, splayed fingers and hands limp. The old man and the cop
cuffed him, had him sit on the ground cross-legged, on his own
hands.

"Boy, you are as dumb as shit," Willows said, helping Ben up. "He
would've probably smashed your face in like a fat kid eating a
cookie for jumping him like that. You know he almost got an extra
five onto his sentence for beating some Aryan brother to a pulp?"
Ben grinned, rubbing his jaw, brushing his shirt off. "Guy swiped
reefer and speed Ricky here had, then offered to sell it back for a
HJ. Almost broke his neck, didn't you boy?" Rick said nothing,
sitting in the darkening yard.

"So why didn't he?" Ben asked, breathing in through his nose deeply, trying to get the pain in his sides and back to calm down. "Get the five, I mean."

Willows passed the shock stick to the uniform, who held it like it was a broadsword. "Oh, the Nazi shitkicker didn't press charges, they could barely get him to admit anything had happened at all. You know how they are in there, deaf and blind, everyone just constantly falls down the stairs on the way to chow."

"You know, you and the uniform could've stepped in sooner," Ben said, retrieving Rick's backpack, zipping it open. "Ahh but then I wouldn't have gotten to see the show, now would I? He's had a hard-on for you ever since the trial you know, knew it was you got him set up. He's not as stupid as you think." Ben fished out a few bundles of cash, a box of heavy-caliber bullets, and a strange-looking, heavy handgun, black unfinished metal and fake wooden grip, barrel long and off somehow. "What the hell is this?"

"Mateba autorevolver," Willows said. "Fancy shit, probably stashed along with that cash from before the trial. Fires like a Glock or a Colt, but loads like a six-shooter. Barrel's suspended to be lower to minimize recoil. Figured he'd have some flashy piece like that, I don't think they even sell them that much in the States." The three of them dragged Rick to his feet, put him in the back of the black-and-white with his gun and bag of cash and clothes in the trunk. "So, you need a ride back to New York?"

"Yeah, actually," Ben said. "I had to cab it here from the train station, my buddy was already gone."

"Well, tough shit," Willows said, "I'm gonna be neck-deep with Jersey cops to get this gentleman back to New York. I just wanted to see if you're stuck here, in case we need a witness." He got in beside the uniformed cop, rolling the window down. "You know, I wonder just how good he is, operating-wise, he found you pretty quick. I know you're not the brightest or bravest bulb in the box, but you ain't that sloppy to let him find you."

"Unless I left a sham note to lure him here, figuring he'd break into my place, see it, come here, thinking he could roll up on me and try to strong-arm me with that space-age six-shooter." Ben grinned, and in the back seat of the car he could see Rick realize that he'd been lured. "Thanks for answering the phone when I called, by the way. It took me an hour of being on hold for someone to be able to dig up your name as his parole officer."

"Ahh, wanting the real police to come and save the day for you, PI?"

"I've never admitted to being particularly brave," Ben grinned, scratching at his messy hair, "just sort of ballsy."

The old cop didn't say anything, just stared at him. "Kids these days," he muttered, rolling the window up. The cruiser rolled away, lights flashing, burping a single siren blip, disappearing around the corner. Ben watched them drive away, walked back to the house, went inside through the backyard, the fireflies bright now, dancing like little green lightning flashes against the black of the night.

"Cul De Sac"

I CANNOT BELIEVE WHAT that asshole did! Franks thought, driving past the gate and guardhouse at the beginning of the neighborhood, headed towards his street. He jerked the wheel hard to take the next turn, and he could hear people on their lawns yell and admonish him as he drove past. *Fuck 'em, I'm not here for that much longer anyway,* he told himself in his head, driving home from work. Just how long DID it take for fake passports and credit cards, anyway?

The sun was going down, and Franks did have to admit to himself as he pulled closer to his cul-de-sac that it did make the neighborhood look pretty, bathed in bright red sunlight. He slowed the car down to a crawl, knowing his annoying neighbors would be knocking on his front door not fifteen minutes after he'd been home if he came into the cul-de-sac at any speed over a mile an hour.

Fucking suburbanite shits, I can't wait until I'm outta here. Once the papers come, so long Maryland, hello Chicago! Franks fumbled with the garage door opener, a skill that the greasy and wily Ponzi scheme mastermind-in-hiding could never master while balancing driving at the same time. *East Coast's too hot for me, good thing I managed to get lost before the trial. Midwest might be good for me.*

The garage rumbled open, slowly, and Franks rolled the car in quickly, already seeing one of his neighbors approaching him. He hit the button again, and the door began to slide down, the nosy fucker yelling something at him. The door clanked down with a metallic thud and Franks was already inside his house though, dropping everything on the living room floor and heading to the fridge. "I need a beer," he said out loud, letting his frustration seep into his tone now that he was alone.

"Hey, Leon."

Leon Franks nearly pissed his pants jumping up in terror, turning around to find Ben Miles sitting on his couch, reading a paperback novel.

Warn me, Franks thought, thinking back to his neighbor trying to catch him before his garage door closed. The asshole was actually trying to help me, warn me.

"I'm assuming you're thinking of your nosy neighbor, who didn't buy my 'representative of a dead rich relative' story and was trying to let you know that someone scummy-looking like me was asking about you." Ben dog-eared the paperback, looking at the high-class conman he'd spent two weeks trying to track down. "It doesn't matter, to be totally honest, I got an actual warrant and everything. You know they were gonna throw a party for you? Then turn you over themselves after the party? Great employees."

"I-I, I know," Franks stuttered, "I overheard, panicked, took off."

"Couldn't have been too much panic, you managed to empty out all of your emergency cash drops, a fake ID that would last a year or so until tax time, and that fancy A-R Spyder car you got stuck in storage at the place behind the Chicken Wing a few miles away."

Ben stood up, grabbing a jacket from the chair where it'd dropped, slipping it on and sliding the book into an inner pocket. "Come on, man, let's go. I got a car waiting."

"B-but you're not even my bondsman, you got no authority over me!" Franks began to circle in the kitchenette, and Ben let his hands come out of the coat's pockets, ready. "I could call the cops right now, or scream for help!"

Ben sighed, reaching into his jacket pocket, pulling out a wad of paper. "See? What'd I say? I have a warrant for you, your bondsman hired me to do the physical work here, track you down. I might as well be the judge, because if I had to I could drag you straight to the courthouse, and they could throw you in a cell there to wait." Ben could tell that the renegade financier conman was close to bolting. "Instead, how about we go to the Holiday Inn, get a room, go back to the city tomorrow. Look," he started to slowly walk in time, following Franks pace around the house, "You know you might not even get jail time, right? This is small-time shit, maybe country-club minimum-security for a few months, and after that? Book deal? TV deal?"

Franks stopped pacing and wringing his hands at that. "R-really? TV?"

"Yeah, sure, why not? I'm sure you'll get a CNN interview, your lawyer's probably fielding calls in his office right now for book and movie rights." He headed towards Franks, nudging to the door. "Come on man, if we leave now we can hit up happy hour somewhere befo..."

There was a loud and insistent rapping at the front door. "Leon? Leon, you in there? Are you alright? There was a strange man ask…"

Suddenly Franks bolted, pushing past Ben to get to the front door, throwing it open, bolting outside, sending the neighbor sprawling into the front lawn. "Jesus," Ben sighed, taking off after him. "I hate running!" he yelled, leaping over the down neighbor.

The cul-de-sac was large, almost ten houses with expansive lawns and large, unfenced or partially-fenced back yards, so Ben could see the frantic man running between two houses into their shared yard across the street. He chased after him, hearing people yell, and his peripheral vision was full of pointing and staring as he bolted after the surprisingly-fast older man.

Oh wait, that's right he remembered, Franks used to run the New York City Marathon every year, rich and full of himself and wanting to show off. "Holy fuck," Ben could barely manage to run two blocks without dying, panted, rounding a corner behind a house and feeling his foot sink into a wet puddle of mostly mud. He almost fell and tumbled, seeing a shocked woman tending to her garden. "Sorry ma'am, federal fugitive chase," he said, only partially lying as he took off at full speed again, down the slope of the backyard towards the edge of the prefab neighborhood property, the swampy tree line marking off a wall against the highway that Ben could faintly hear as the sun was going down.

Shit, it's almost dark. And he already had lost Franks, knew that if he stopped again he'd be gone and probably crossing the highway or maybe even looping around back to his house to grab his car, cash, something, to run again. Frank might be a twitchy little shit, but he was a professional money-swindler and had run like a pro, better than some actual pros Ben knew. Under house arrest after getting caught the first time trying to fly to Florida, he went out the front door in a stupid disguise, claiming to have been building maintenance. US Marshals had looked for a week, couldn't find him.

Somewhere faintly, he could hear cars squeal and sirens. Cops. Maybe private security, but probably real cops. Great.

Ben had tracked down Franks' girlfriend, threw the info and how much money the weasel had been blowing on her, at Franks' wife and son. They rolled over on him quickly, especially when Ben mentioned he knew the girl, who he'd been watching, was packing up, like someone was coming to get her. Someone who should have been planning to pick up his family instead.

Suddenly, he could hear a splashing and crashing, and he took off in the general direction of the noise. The light was dying now, almost gone, and Ben stopped for a moment, fumbling in his pocket for his iPhone, letting the bright light of the flashlight application illuminate the ground at his feet.

"Jesus Christ, over here!" Franks was yelling, and Ben found him sprawled amongst a mess of broken branches and tree trunks, his leg laid out and twisted, his clothing ripped. "I think I broke my leg, man! Look what you did to me!"

"Me?" Ben laughed, holding his phone up to see, feeling his feet slip and slide on the muddy ground. "I didn't do jack-shit!" Jesus, no wonder he feel like he did, running full speed. He could almost see Franks covered in mud, he'd probably gone flying along the sopping-wet ground when he feet gave way under him. "What'd you do, hit the top of the hill making a turn, slip?"

"Y-Yeah," Franks sobbed, trying to wriggle free of the refuse. It was a little pathetic to be honest, and Ben almost giggled. "Totally going to loop around, give me the slip, go back to your house while I fumble around in the dark?" Ben looked up the hill and could see, faintly, the search lights of the police. He could still feel the faint burn in his lungs from his run chasing Franks, and he breathed deep of the night air, rank from the swamp but cool enough to make his chest feel better. "Jeez, I need to get in shape" he muttered, to no one in particular besides the dark.

All of a sudden he felt a hand on his ankle, and Franks was clawing at his leg, trying to climb up by dragging Ben down, Ben dropping the glowing iPhone. "What the fuck is wrong with you?" he yelled, trying to kick at the downed man, maintain his balance. Franks didn't answer, clawing and pulling at Ben's pants and trying to get a grip on his pockets, either working to drag the PI down into the mud or pull himself up, Ben couldn't tell as he fought to keep his balance on the uneven wet ground and fight at Franks' muddy slippery hands. He gave up, letting himself fall back into the mud, hit the ground with a wet THUD, seeing any progress Franks made climbing up him crash as the two of them went down, rolling and crashing back into the mess of broken wood.

"We could've gone for Happy Hour at the Holiday Inn!" Ben yelled, trying to pull himself, slowly, up the hill out of the brambles of branches and tree trunks, and kicking at Franks, mostly ineffectively, for good measure. "Happy Hour! Bourbon, easy waitresses! Then a jail probably nicer than my apartment! YOU

FUCKING ASSHOLE!" Ben yelled, trying to prop himself up on his elbows in the mud, trying to catch his breath. "I-I panicked! I'm sorry, oh God, it really hurts man, c'mon help me!" Franks cried.

Ben looked up the hill, could see search lights and men who looked like police, probably private security, peering down the hill. "You know what? No," he said, letting himself lay there on his back in the mud. "Let's just wait." He fumbled around, found the iPhone, and lifted the glowing screen up for the police lights to find.

Running

The

Train

01.

"That'll be $4.50."

"Jesus."

"Sorry 'old man,'" the girl said, grinning.

Ben slid the $5 across the counter, walking away as she dropped the change into the jar. "Thanks!" she half-yelled at him, and he couldn't tell if she was being sarcastic or not. He sat down at one of the tables inside the near-empty coffee shop, nursing the iced coffee and flipping through his smart phone.

"I always thought you were some sort of hipster," someone said, sitting down across from him. "Iced coffee?"

Ben grinned, scratching at his stubble. "It's hot, what can I say." Kalli Kiliaris sighed. "OK, so what are we doing here? I actually had clients coming in today. You know what those are, right?"

Ben sucked on the straw of the iced coffee. "Very funny." He looked out of the corner of one eye at the only other patron in the store, an older woman furiously working at a cell phone, scribbling periodically into a notebook she'd pull out of her pants pocket. Kalli followed his gaze out of habit, and nodded. "So, you aren't totally useless."

"Not entirely," he said low. "She tends to roam around, last week she was at the Dunkin' Donuts every morning for hours during the daytime. Eventually someone asked her to go, I think they thought she's a drug dealer."

"You want the phone?" Kalli asked, equally as low. The far more competent PI, grafter, and bondswoman, she had employees, didn't work out of her personal residence, had an office, paid taxes on time, and didn't dress like a 20-something actor who played teenagers for a living. Ben could see her hands tense up into fists, then relax.

"The notebook," he murmured. "Phone's a really expensive throwaway, but the notebook's the key. I'm sure she's got a backup, but I know she doesn't synch the backup with the master too often, the master's at least a month ahead of the backup. I need that month."

"Mother?" Kalli murmured back, fully into it now. Ben smiled on the inside. Kalli was a good, but spent too much time tracking wayward husbands, bail-jumping corporate types, and following money trails. He knew sometimes she missed smaller stuff, the weirder stuff he got, so he could always call her up, get her to ditch a client meeting, help him out. "Yeah," he said, putting the iced coffee down, pushing it to the side, half-empty now and mostly melted ice. "Mom called me up, had a suspicion. Then the kid doesn't come home one night, & here I am."

"Jesus," Kalli said. "So," she laid her hand on his, seeing the woman eyeball them, suspicious already possibly. "Want to make it loud? Or just fast?"

"Both," Ben muttered, then jerked his hand away. "Jesus Christ, what the fuck is wrong with you!" He yelled loudly, seeing the barista look over at them, the woman as well. "I told you, this was it!"

"But I thought we had something!" Kalli screamed suddenly, sagging her shoulders, getting up, standing over him, playing the part. "I-I thought you loved m…"

"Oh get the fuck off it!" Ben stood up too, and pushed, sending Kalli flying across the coffee shop, into the woman's table, sending it tilting over, everything spilling over. "Leave me the hell alone, bitch!" Ben stormed out of the coffee shop, slamming the door hard behind him, out and down the block, around the corner, across the street, and into an alley between a deli and an apartment building. He could hear yelling, and a minute later, Kalli bolted around the corner, down the block, past him. He took off after her, followed her down another block, around another corner, found her catching her breath, grinning, on a bus stop bench. He sat down next to her, and she handed him the notebook, a small moleskin wrapped in rubber bands, with "2012-II" in silver pen on the spine. "You are the best," he said, before she slugged him, hard, in the hip.

Ben almost slid off the bench from the force of it. "Owww! What the fuck was that for?" Kalli grinned now, maliciously. "That push hurt, asshole. I still remember how to trip and slip on purpose, you know. You didn't have to push that hard."

Ben rubbed his hip, grimaced. "Yeah, yeah, sorry. So, you wanna see what this leads to? Or you got some fancy-ass clients to schmooze still?" He opened up the notebook, looking at the pages, filled with scrawl. "I'm pretty sure Pete can crack this today if I bring him enough Chinese food."

"Do you really think it's her? The Sunnyside Madame?"

Ben flipped through pages. "I'm not sure. I know she's running high school girls, conning them, letting them get in deep, thinking it's a game, and then when they make a fuss, grabbing them, but the big Queen of Queens? I always assumed she'd be Chinese, to be honest. I don't know about you, but I don't think that lady was exactly the Dragon Lady. Pardon the racism." The Sunnyside Madame was an urban legend, running half of the call girls in the outer boroughs of New York City, supposedly out of Sunnyside, a neighborhood of Queens known for Irish and Romanian immigrants, as well as young hip couples who wanted to avoid the high prices of Brooklyn. The only people who would seriously consider her real tended to be bondsmen who would find themselves bonding out high-priced call girls who had fancy lawyers and paid with wire transfers, something weird in a mostly-cash business. "So, you down."

"Yeah, sure. This could be interesting."

.02

Three hours later, they were in Flushing, Chinese takeout piled up in a cramped apartment, and Ben, Kalli, and long-haired, code-breaking anarchist home-cook savant Peter Connelly hunched over the notebook. "You know," Peter said, pushing duct-taped, thick black-framed glasses up his nose, "this really isn't that hard. It's number replacement, pretty much any idiot could figure this out. Even you. So what's this supposed to be, anyway?"

"Some madam's daybook, dates, names, prices, the usual." Kalli said, standing up, walking over to pick at the crab Rangoon out on the table. "Ben thinks it's the Sunnyside Madame, she grabbed some girl who got wise and wanted out."

"No shit?" Pete said, looking at Ben. "So this is like, a real case?"

"I have real cases!"

"Not like this, you don't." Pete finished staring at the last page, transferred some numbers over to the large legal-sized sheets of paper he was scrawling more legible names and different numbers onto. "Okay, I think I got the last month or two. You know, I think you might be onto something. There's another column of numbers here, see?" He pointed to the first column in the translations, a set of five numbers that changed periodically as you went down the list. "What do those look like?" Ben stared, it not making sense, until about a third of the way into the second page.

11354.

"Holy shit." 11354, the postal code for Flushing. "They're postal codes, she's tracking her own patterns so her phone can't be tracked."

"Is she using a throwaway?" Pete said, and Kalli was on her own phone with her agency, talking low but urgently. "Yeah," Ben said, "one of those pay-as-you go smartphones, she switches up every few weeks." He looked at the list, then fished his own notebook out of his back pocket, flipping through battered pages, consulted quickly. "Doesn't synch up with the change in codes, though."

Kalli hung her phone up. "Makes sense. Ben, if this is really her, she's been working since the seventies, she is one-hundred percent a pro, probably has hookups with the Chinese and Koreans to bring girls in, and maybe even plants in the schools to get girls from there in with her. Never mind the muscle she could get on us, and guys who'd love to smash some PI's nosy fucking face in considering the money she's dealing in." She sat back down, continued talking. "I hate to be crude too, but you know that girl's probably in a squat somewhere, high, with guys running the train on her for $20 a pop. How long has it been, two weeks?"

"Almost three," Ben said, frowning, gnawing at his thumbnail. "Shit."

Kalli pulled out her phone, flipped through the touchscreen, passed it to him. "I called my office, they're sending someone over now. My lawyer, too. Here, call her mom. Tell her the truth."

Ben took the phone, didn't look at it, finally handing it back. "No, not yet."

"Ben…"

"No, not yet. I'd rather wait until I know for sure."

"Know for sure what? That she's dead from an OD to keep her quiet?"

Pete coughed, adjusting his glasses. "She has a point, man. Here," he handed Ben a scrap of paper, "this is her name, right? This is the last address she had in here attached to that name, it was maybe four days ago? The dates switch sometimes, I'm trying to figure that part out."

Ben snatched the paper, headed out the door. "Gimme a while, okay?" Kalli nodded, putting her phone back up to her ear."

Outside the apartment building, Ben passed three men, two in work shirts and arms full of notebooks and laptops, the third a suit. "You're Ben Miles," the suit said. He handed him two cards, one Kalli's, the other from Kadinsky, Kolins, Smith. "This could make your name, you know, busting this. Have the police been called yet?"

"No," Ben said, handing the cards back. "They're upstairs, just buzz to get in." He took off before the lawyer could answer, crossing the street and around the corner, past the deli, into the drugstore next door, down towards the back. "Bathroom?" he asked the lone pharmacist there, bored, reading a magazine. She looked up, "You gonna buy something?" He sighed, throwing a dollar at her and picking up a candy bar from the counter. She handed him a key, pointing towards the far corner.

The bathroom here had a side door leading to the storeroom and back loading dock, and he opened that door up, praying it wasn't rigged to an alarm. He'd been in here once before, and the instant he left Pete's place and saw the two technicians from Kalli's office, knew one of them was one of her guys, meant to tail him, try to keep this whole thing organized. This would make her name, for sure, and she was enough of a friend to know that if left alone, he'd probably get his ribs broken trying to go about this on his own.

There was no alarm, and he slipped out into the back lot, letting the heavy iron door slam closed behind him. He hit the curb right as a bus pulled up, and leapt on. It pulled away with a rumble and hiss, and he could see the fake tech bolt out the back loading door, standing at the curb looking pissed.

"Amateur," Ben said, feeding his MetroCard into the machine, sitting down.

"Hey, buddy," the bus driver said as the bus slowed at a light, "your card's no good. Try again."

.03

Spring nights in the Bronx were usually slightly humid, the nearness of the bay that the Throgs Neck crossed back into Queens letting the sea tint the air. It was fainter as Ben got off the subway at Pelham Bay, the middle of eastern Bronx, but enough. He walked down from the elevated train, down back along the tracks, turned into a small building that could have been a house if not for the sign bolted to the bars over one front window.

He knew Kalli had a place up here that she used and wouldn't be averse to asking questions, especially not once he used the credit card he'd lifted from her purse. The sign read CAR RENTAL TAXI SERVICE in block letters, the paint of the last E peeling slightly.

He walked what used to have been the living room, now a waiting room with a desk and chairs set up, maps pinned to the wall. The older Hispanic man in a baggy t-shirt at the desk on the phone, hanging up as he came in. "Ben?"

"Yeah?" Instantly wary, unsure.

"Miss K said you'd be by," the man said, "she called, figured you'd be up here looking for a car for the day. And not to worry about paying with her card, we'll just put it on her account. So," the older man said, getting up from the desk, stretching his arms and revealing faded old prison-style tattoos peeking out from under his sleeves, "where do you need to go? For a friend of Miss K? I'll take you."

Ben handed him the slip of paper Pete had given him, and the old man frowned. "You sure? This isn't the nicest place for a white boy like you. You're not packing, are you?"

"No, can't stand 'em. Look, you can just drop me off, circle around, if you're worried."

He laughed, handing the address back to Ben. "My man, you think I got to worry?" He went to the desk, fumbled in a drawer, and came back with car keys and what looked like an old leather sap and civilian-model taser. Both entirely illegal in the state of New York. "Miss K, she told me this is about some little girl?"

"Yeah," Ben fished around in his pockets, pulled out a snapshot from his wallet, a high-school profile picture. He handed it to the man. "She's seventeen, running wild, in over her head."

The man handed the picture back. "No excuse, angel like that. She's a baby. Rican?" Ben nodded, putting the picture back into a pocket, then walking over to compare the address to the map of the Bronx against the far wall. "This is?" He tapped at one spot.

"Yeah. I have three at home, I'd do a stretch no problem for them. I tell you now, we're up there, don't hesitate to deck one o'them, show 'em who's boss. Miss K's lawyer'll get us out of what we need if the cops show up. I know you're some kind of clumsy chickenshit..."

"Hold on, what? Did she tell you that?" Ben stopped. They went outside, about into the battered but heavy-looking black Corolla parked by the fire hydrant. The other man grinned, unlocking the trunk, fishing out a new set of plates, ducking down with a pocketknife he'd made appear from his pocket, replacing the plates.

"Yeah, but it's cool, man." He moved smoothly, dumping the old plates into the open trunk, tightening the last few screws, moving to the front of the car to replace the plates there. "There'll be guys there, ya know? Not workin' for 'em, but just watchin', acting like they watch the area. Just be cool, act like we know where we're going." He got up from the front of the car, tossed the other plate into the trunk, slammed it shut. "I' tellin' you this 'cause you're an idiot white guy with a big mouth, Miss K says."

Ben shrugged as the two of them got into the car. "She's probably right."

The older man put the taser and sap on the floor at Ben's feet on the passenger side. "I'm Pedro," he said as the car fired to life and the radio blared, a Mets game screaming to life as they pulled away from the curb, silent.

.04

The car slowed down, parking in the bare dirt lot that signaled the end of the road, right at the water's edge. The Throgs Neck bridge and barge lights cast odd shadows on the ground, with barely any lights from the last few houses at the edge there, right where the tarmac of the street turned into the hard-packed dirt of the water's edge. Pedro and Ben sat in the car, lights off, watching the last two houses. Ben furiously manned his phone, Kalli and Pete streaming information at him that the rest of the notebook and Kalli's lawyer had found out.

"You're like a teenage girl with that, man," Pedro said, content to sit and watch. The street was utterly deserted, every house but one dark, and on the other, a single solitary older man in a rocking chair, buried in a paper, a porch light on above him. The phone buzzed again.

"Cops will be here in an hour or so, they want to know which house. What the hell does that mean? It's the one with the address!" Ben went to point, but the other man shoved his hand down. "Stay still, man. You wanna get made?"

"Made? No one's out here!"

The driver sighed, nudged at the old man on the porch of the other house. "He and that paper haven't moved since we got here two hours ago, not even turning the page. He probably thinks I'm your trick or somethin', you're hustling. Only reason no one's come out of the other house with a bat or a piece to get us goin'. Besides, we don't know which of the two'll be the actual one, which one's the one they use to keep an eye on the street."

"So what are we waiting for?"

Suddenly, they saw the front door open of the house with the old man, and a nervous-looking young man in a suit, white, came out, looking around, walked quickly up the block towards a parked car. "That. I thought you were some sorta private eye?" Pedro got out of the car, indicated for Ben to bring the taser and sap. "You should let Miss K know which house."

Ben hurriedly tapped at the iPhone and rushed to catch up with Pedro, handing him the sap and taser.

"How you get any work done, you didn't notice this guy?" Pedro asked, striding onto the porch, swinging the sap hard onto the wrist of the old man, who leapt up surprisingly agile from his seat, and

Ben heard the soft "crack" of something breaking. "How you ever get paid, man?"

Ben pushed the front door open hard, feeling it resist, and pushed again harder, feeling something or someone slump down below it. "I get by on being pretty," he said. There was no one else on the ground floor. Pedro slid in, and the two of the propped the door closed again, throwing the bolt and hearing the howling of the outside watchman bringing a slew of more voices, banging on the door. "I hear that," Pedro said, and a hand punched through the window next to the door. He grabbed the wrist, hitting it with the taser's prongs, and the two men heard a hideous scream from outside.

"We totally didn't think this through, did we." The downstairs was barren, just a bare kitchen with a table and two chairs, takeout bags everywhere. The other rooms were covered in tags, with a few blankets and mattresses scattered around.

Pedro shrugged, "Nah, man, it's fine. There's prolly a back door leads to the back of another house, a bolthole just in case. Go upstairs, get what we came for, see if she's here. I'm cool. Call my office when you get a block away, tell 'em where you are and that you're with Miss K, they'll come get you."

Ben nodded, taking the stairs up two at a time. "Later man!" It stank on the second floor, a dirty bathroom stench that he knew meant one thing; the house was a den most of the time. He could hear hard thumps and the occasional crack of the taser.

Ben pushed open one door, and nearly wretched. Half a dozen junkies, the smell of blood and piss and burnt opiates. He went down to the next door, second of three, pushed it open. A bed, a table with chair, a girl's sweater, and a nightstand table. He yanked the drawer of the nightstand open hard, condoms and breath mints scattering. The window was open, and Ben found a nail file and screws on the windowsill. She'd probably worked the screws all day to try to get them out. "Clever girl." He looked out the window, saw the half-destroyed wooden trellis against the back of the house, probably for roses from decades ago. It was splintered and worn. She'd climbed down.

The sounds from the downstairs got close all of a sudden, and Ben ran out into the hallway. The final door was just a closet full of clothing, girls' shirts, purses, wallets, skirts. He ran back downstairs, turning the corner fast as he hit the bottom of the stairs. Out of the corner of his eye, Pedro was at the front window, glass everywhere, bellowing in Spanish.

"Hey old man, come on!"

Quick for his age, Pedro was a step ahead of Ben, in the kitchen, throwing the fridge aside with a surprising strength, exposing the back door. "Where I always hid it," he said, seeing Ben's surprise. They threw it open, taking off into the backyard, across the narrow grass alley, into the yard of another house in an instant. A light went on, and they bolted around the house, past a car in a driveway, out into the street.

.05

"You call her mom?"

Ben grimaced, feeling his leg grind and pop as he sat in Kalli's office. "Oh shit, needed that." He'd fallen hard as he and Kalli's man Pedro had run from the house, and the big Hispanic man had half-dragged him to a deli ten blocks away, where they had called Kalli and Pete, as well as the car company, making sure someone would go by after the police raided the den, found the half-asleep junkies, a busted window, a living room full of bangers with piss-stained pants from a taser making them void their bowels, and a closet full of clothing taken from girls. "Yeah, called her this morning, told her everything so far. She's got half her family combing around, hoping she's gonna come home. Who knows, she might. Where the hell did you dig Pedro up from, anyway?"

Kalli grinned. "Trade secret. Some of us are actually good at this job, remember?" She passed him a cup of coffee her secretary brought in. Ben smiled at the girl, and she smiled back.

"Hey, asshole, quit hitting on my niece." Kalli smacked his shoulder. "Listen, I gave everything we had to the cops so far, my lawyer's idea. I know your man Pete hates the boys in blue, so we moved everything over hear, made it seem like my guys broke the code from the notebook, which we 'found,' not stole."

"Probably for the best," Ben said, pulling his phone out of his pocket, the battered iPhone vibrating. "It's her. Yes?" He held the phone up, and Kalli saw his face relax. He held the phone away from his ear, grinning as a slew of Spanish blared out. "Yes, yes, you're welcome. No, it was my pleasure. Remember to recommend us." He hung up, took a sip of the coffee. "She showed up an hour ago, dopesick. Bus driver in Pelham Bay found her, called the number she gave him, and one of her uncles picked her up."

Ben sagged in the chair, feeling tension drain out of him slowly as every muscle uncoiled and his "She'd been on downers I guess, which is weird for them to use pills like that. She hoarded them enough she could stay awake and work the window loose, get out."

"Clever kid," Kalli said, sipping from her coffee, attention now pulled by whatever was on the computer monitor on her desk.

Ben frowned. "I know, which is weird. I didn't see any pills at the house, and a place like that catered to needle jockeys. But there were no needles or spoons or anything in that room." He got up, walked over to the window of the office, stared out at the street below. "So what's your lawyer buddy say about the notebook, the Sunnyside Madame thing?"

"Huh? Oh, just that we should've called the cop, yadda yadda yadda..."

"Do you know how many nonwhite teenage girls run away from home in New York City each year?" Ben said, still staring out the window. "The amount of missing persons reports is staggering. Trust me, first thing I did was go down, check out the file on her. They almost laughed at me." He thunked his head against the glass lightly. "Just, something doesn't add up about that house address we got from the notebook. A single room with a girl for guys to go see, but otherwise just shit for junkies everywhere? And what about that closet full of shit?"

"The cops said a lot of it matched up with missing persons cases, actually, mostly young girls that probably ended up as pros in that house, or similar ones." Kalli pushed away from the desk, watching Ben from her chair. "Man, you gotta let this go, I thought your client was the mom, bringing the girl back? How did you even think the Sunnyside Madame had anything to do with this?"

"I saw her lurking a lot in the girl's neighborhood, when I first started, right after she disappeared. Followed her around, realized she was running girls in various apartments as well as email appointments from her phone. OK, no biggie, lots of working ladies in the city, but then I see her one day, the last day I tell myself I'm gonna tail her, talking to someone. A couple of kids, guy and a girl. He was older, actin' like her boyfriend. She was maybe fifteen?"

"Recruiter."

"Exactly. Now a regular old pro like this lady? She wouldn't bother with amateur recruiting, not unless she had more going on that just maybe a dozen girls in apartments in Manhattan, operating off of a website and some email addresses. Figured there had to be a connection, so I stuck around." Ben was pacing the office, thumped down into the chair, let one foot lean against the desk. "But now? Now I'm not so sure." Kalli leaned forward, swatting at his foot as he continued. "I feel like maybe something's up with this house, like it was a sham? A blind? I don't know, I'm fuckin' going bonkers."

"You could talk to the girl?"

"If she's really in on it, she's not gonna admit anything, not after everyone that got involved to 'rescue' her. And if she's not? I'd feel like total scum, coming down on her after an ordeal like that." Ben stood up suddenly. "I'm gonna go nose around, check a few other things out."

"Call Pedro if you need help not getting kicked in the face," Kalli said, going back to the computer screen as Ben walked through the outer office to the elevators, down back onto the street. He headed for the nearest subway staircase, leapt up towards the elevated N train.

.06

It looked different in the daylight somehow, and not just because of the police tape everywhere and broken front window and porch, courtesy of Pedro's holding the line that night. It seemed softer almost, a little less harsh and painful to look at. The patrol car that had been floating around the block finally disappeared, and Ben slipped back into the house from the backyard he'd run through that night. The fridge was still on its side, smashed against the far wall, untouched.

It almost looked pathetic in the light of day, and Ben picked his way carefully through the mess, gingerly as if everything might crumble at his touch. The signs of the cops tearing the place to shit were everywhere, with every drawer ripped open and every cabinet doorless. The upstairs room full of smoke and shit and the burnt smell of opiates and filthy junkies was now almost alarmingly empty and large, crushed pipes, cracked needles, and a shattered mirror underfoot. The burnt-spoon-and-shit smell was in the air still, but just the absence of people aired it out significantly.

The closet at the far end was empty, every piece of clothing tagged and tied back to a missing person's case, just like Kalli had said. That only left the middle door, the girl's room with the screwed-shut windows she'd pried open with a nail file she'd gotten her hands on after cheeking all the meds they had her on to keep her docile. Pried the window open, waited until right after one more john so they wouldn't get suspicious, and then the instant the door closed behind him, out she went. Pretty daring. Pretty clever.

If it was true.

He leaned out and over the still-open window again, looking down at the trellis and the bushes below. How big was this girl again? He couldn't remember what her mom and said and the only visual reference had been that high school picture. How much could a seventeen-year-old weigh anyway? Not much, not enough to seriously get hurt jumping even halfway down into the shrubbery.

"This is stupid" he muttered aloud, resting his head on the windowsill. I'm probably just overthinking this to shit. He opened his eyes, staring at the wood of the windowsill, got up, and slammed the window closed.

The holes weren't there.

He stopped, dropped to his knees, nose inches from the floor.

Ben went through everything again, even though, he admitted to himself, the cops did a good job tearing the whole house apart. Guys usually thought they were being really clever hiding stuff inside nooks and crannies and hidden panels or drawers. Too many spy movies. But if the cops, or anyone for that matter, really wanted to find it? And didn't care who knew they'd been looking? They'd find it. Hammers to the walls, knives to every seam in anything fabric, stuffing and insulation raining down stairwells as clothing and furniture were shaken out.

Ben had once tagged along with a friend, a prison guard, while they were shaking down cells, and the intensity of the searches was alarming. Mirrors on angles, magnets, adhesive dissolvers to undo glue and fake plaster cover, even their Kevlar-clad hands, covering every square inch of the cell, with everything the prisoner had dumped out into the hallway. "You can't be too careful," his friend had said afterwards over beers, "I once found a segmented razorblade, eight pieces long, in the waistband of a pair of shorts. Bastard ran wire through it, could just undo the seam, slide it out, pull the wire taunt, and it'd lock into place, almost six inches long."

But cons in prison always managed to get new stuff, hide new weapons and drugs. It'd get found eventually, but they always managed to get it. Ben tapped against every piece of wood against the wall and floor he could see, every angle in a piece of metal underneath the frame of the bed, every inch of the battered nightstand. His fingers scrambled as he wormed his way around on the floor, and his nail caught on something. A loose piece of floorboards, barely three inches square, flew up on a hinge. A phone jack for a land line stared up at Ben, and he smiled.

He intensified his search through the room, knocking everything over he could, feeling at the corners, reaching up to try to feel at the ceilings, reaching on his tiptoes, while standing up on the nightstand. *There's a phone in here, somewhere.*

The nightstand sagged for a brief second as he stood there, and with an almost soggy splintering sound, it gave way, Ben's foot going clean through the wood as he tumbled down, falling hard onto the ground. He felt the floorboards shudder as he fell straight onto his back, staring up at the ceiling. The dust settled, and he groaned, feeling every muscle in his back tight with agony and bruising already.

"Christ!"

He looked around, coughing, feeling the remnants of the stand on his foot, and he shook it, feeling it still awkwardly clinging around his ankle like a wooden toy bear trap. He pulled his leg up, slowly, towards his hands, hoping to pry it off, and cold plastic met his fingers. A phone. A goddamn phone, hidden inside the nightstand somewhere.

Clever kid.

"Hey who's that!" a voice bellowed from downstairs, and feet pounded against the stairs, someone heavy coming closer. Ben scrambled, pushing the door closed to the room, throwing his own body against it, keeping whoever it was from pushing it in.

Shit.

"Seriously, fucking open up, it's the police!" the voice yelled, and then he heard the static of a radio. Shit shit shit, it was the cruiser. The cops had probably come back, come inside to snoop around or probably use the john. Shit.

"Ah, fuck it."

He got up, letting the door slide suddenly open, the remnants of the phone and nightstand still tangled on his foot, the cops fingertips brushing against the collar of his shirt, and dove through the closed window, the glass shattering against his hands and head, breaking the smoothness of the motion, and he tumbled over once, twice, hitting the ground in the shrubbery, rolling, feeling glass in his arms and hands and hair, up, kicking the mess of the wood and plastic free from his leg finally, taking off down and around the corner, the cop peering out the window in amazement.

.07

"What do you mean you found a phone? And why are you panting?"

Ben sighed, slumping against the fifth pay phone he'd hit up, the only one working so far in the blocks he'd run since diving out the window. He'd been moving nonstop since. "A phone! The girl I was searching for? That had been in that room and escaped? She had a phone in there with her!"

At the other end of the line, Pete was silent. "Man, if you're saying what I think you're saying…"

"I don't know what I'm saying, I just know that there's something else going on."

"You sure?"

"If she was being doped up and used at that house, why would there be a hidden phone?"

"Speaking of which, why aren't you on your cell calling me? You know I hate numbers I don't know." Ben winced. Pete was notoriously paranoid, it took far too many tried to get him to pick up. Ben felt in his pocket, the shattered remains of the touchscreen phone in there from where he'd fallen on it. "Long story. Anyway, like I'm saying, it doesn't make any sense, there being a room for a girl that shouldn't be allowed to leave, much less call anyone, with a phone in it!"

"Maybe the phone was there before she was in there?"

Ben rubbed his face, frowning. "Man, you know guys like this would've scoured that room before throwing her in there, I'm surprised there was even anything other than a bed. I worked a job once, chased some guy into a place like that. Just dope everywhere and a mattress on the floor, they're fucking hovels." Ben looked around nervously, paranoia creeping in as a car's engine could be heard a block or so away. "Look, I gotta talk to you, I'm coming over. Don't tell Kalli if she calls lookin', alright?" Ben hung up the phone before he could hear Pete's answer, letting the dirty plastic receiver clunk down as he drifted up the block, limping slightly, around the corner.

A phone. A hidden phone with a hidden phone line in the house in a room that should have been a cell for a girl being rented out by the quarter-hour. And hidden well, too, it was only sheer fucking luck that he found it, with the rotting frail wood giving way as he stood on it. Otherwise who knew how long the almost ridiculous superspy-style hiding place would have remained, undetected.

Thank God for being out of shape and slightly overweight.

Ben breathed deeply, feeling his ribs flex and stab with pain as he did. Maybe cracked ribs, bruised at the very least. Scrapes, bruises on his one arm, and he could feel a hot wet spot on his face near his jaw line, probably a deep cut. He could hear sirens now, probably the kid cop finally having made up his mind whether or not to call in that someone was in the crime scene and had jumped from a second-story window.

God, that was so stupid, if the bushes hadn't been under the window he could've broken his neck. He felt his gait, irregular, as he kept moving, hoping that the constant movement would make it less noticeable to people around him. He was getting closer to a more populated part of the neighborhood. All it takes is one concerned citizen and he'd be screwed. Gotta keep moving.

The stairs up to the subway appeared suddenly as Ben turned a corner, and he went up, automatically following the stairs to the turnstile, swiping his card, up to the platform. The sirens were faint now, the trail lost into nothingness as the train pulled up with a smooth hiss, Ben collapsing into the cool plastic of the bench across from the doorway, the day finally catching up to him.

A phone. A phone in a room that was made to look like a den for a young high school girl to get doped up and pimped out. A fakeout obviously, the way ancient Egyptian tombs had fake treasure rooms and empty vaults to distract tomb robbers. But why would the girl be there in the first place if she could call, if she wasn't there to turn tricks, too full to the gills on heroin to say no? No one knew the girl was doing anything that'd make her a junkie on her own, and it wasn't like she would be working th…

"Oh, shit." Ben bolted up in his seat on the train, the old man next to him startlingly moving away. Shit, shit, shit. The older woman, young handsome men recruiting high school girls, it's what's always worked. He buys her things, takes her out, takes her to parties, alienates her from family, then friends. They experiment with drugs, her more than him because she's newer at it, and then he goes in for the kill, telling her how she needs to help him so that they can keep getting drugs. And by then, it's too late.

And it's not the only way.

The train shuddered to a stop at the next station, Ben bolting from the train, running down the platform, seeing the lone payphone at the end. "Hey," the voice said at his ear, and Ben turned around as he was moving, on instinct.

The punch to the back of the head was probably the worst, because it sent him sprawling forward due to his own momentum, a blindly-splintering pain radiating at the back of his neck when the fist hit his skin. After that, the kick to his bruised side wasn't so bad, because his head swam and the fall made the injuries from falling from the window act up, making his entire body a mass of nerve signals going off, firing in agony.

"You like looking around our house?" the voice said again, the kicks continuing, even as a new train roared into the station, Ben feeling it shudder and shake the concrete slabs making up the platform. He shook his head, feeling something wet and warm trickle down into his eyes, probably blood, as the voice was close now, kneeling. "Take a break, you know? Or next time remember to bring the big 'Rican with ya." And then it was gone, and Ben coughed hard, feeling the same warm wetness com up in his mouth, and he spit red.

.08

"Ow ow OW!"

"Wow, that Kiliaris lady wasn't kidding, was she?"

"Whu?" Ben groaned as the paramedic swabbed at his head and face. There'd been a scream after the voice, and he'd passed out, waking up with cops and paramedics sitting him up. Including the young cop who'd caught him at the house.

"You know, that you're kind of a pussy." The cops chuckled, and the paramedic grinned as he placed butterfly bandages on Ben's face and scalp. "There you go, no harm, no foul."

"What the fuck is this shit!" Ben said, patting at his head, his face. "No stitches?" He felt the bandages on his head stuck to his hair, matted down already from the blood where his scalp had split open hitting the ground. The young cop grinned. "Whoever hit ya was wearing Kevlar gloves." He held up a police evidence bag, with black-and-stained hi-tech-looking gloves inside. "Fancy padded shit they make for SWAT guys, but anyone can get 'em. Cushioned but also weighed his punches, probably. The only thing you're really gonna need's a goddamn excuse so I don't book the living fuck..."

"That's enough, officer," another voice said, and Ben looked up as the cops and paramedics quieted down at the uniformed suit. He might have had a lieutenant's bars, but Ben could tell a suit with real influence over beat cops and paramedics, especially with Kalli Kiliaris and her lawyer at his elbow. She looked at him with no pity and a little bit of resignation.

"You do realize that guys from the car place have been following you ever since you got off the subway up here, right?" She crouched down in front of him as the paramedic and uniform melted into the background, wordlessly. "Did you really jump from that window?"

Ben nodded, feeling his head swim at the movement against the butterfly bandages and dried sticky blood. "Yeah, I know, stupid to show up, looking for shit at the house, but I go, I gotta…" he wavered for a bit, faltering as he tried to move to get up. "Hold on, you lost a lot of blood. I know, Pete called me." Kalli helped him stand up, her and the lawyer propping him up against the train platform wall. "Look, I got an idea, but you need to rest, take it easy."

"Yeahmmm, tuk'it easy…" Ben slurred, closing his eyes, shaking his head. "Yeah, easy, I promise." He could feel Kalli and the lawyer helping him down to the street level, walking and getting into a waiting car. "Hey man, you look like shit," Pedro said from the front seat as Kalli and Ben drove away, leaving the lawyer on the sidewalk with the lieutenant.

"Thanks," Ben said, rubbing his face. "Jesus, that shit hurts." He felt the soreness in his side from the window jump. "Got anything I can take? Medics didn't give me shit."

"You didn't get shit because you almost got arrested and drugging you before slapping cuffs on you is technically illegal," Kalli said furiously, scrolling through the iPhone. "I can't believe you jumped like that, Ben. Why not just run past him really quickly? That cop would have probably thought you were just a junkie or someone homeless. A guy leaping from the window was just weird enough to warrant the attention you got. Well, from the cops at least." She looked up from the iPhone, showing him the screen. "Was this the guy?"

Ben peered at the small smartphone glass screen, seeing a smooth-cheeked younger man, a mugshot that exuded a level of false cockiness that only money and a family lawyer could buy. "I don't know, could be?" Kalli sighed, pulling the phone back into her inner jacket pocket. "He's a local guy, mostly works in the Bronx so they think he might've been the one whoever owns the house got him on you to keep you away. He's probably been watching it since before the raid, saw you go in, followed you out the back. You probably didn't notice but you made a shit-ton of noise, falling out that window."

Ben sat back in his seat, groaning and gingerly touching at his scalp and face. "Makes sense," he said, sucking air in between his teeth at the pain from even the gentle feelings at the bandages. His side-pain had died down to a dull throb, though this only helped exacerbate the pain in his head and face. "So, what did Pete tell you after I told him not to call you?"

They'd been moving faster than Ben realized, already in Queens over the Whitestone Bridge, outside the car north Queens whizzing by as Pedro maneuvered the car smoothly through end-of-day traffic. "I, uh, I had an idea about what was bugging me about that room." Ben looked out the window. "Look, I think that we might definitely be able to get a step closer to the Sunnyside Madame. I know that that part of this whole thing's stalled out, right?" Kalli didn't say anything, putting the phone away. "Ben…"

"No, no, no! Look, I told you guys I had a strange feeling about it, and I was fucking right! I found-"

"It doesn't matter what you found, Ben! It doesn't fucking matter because you were wrong, there is no Sunnyside Madame, that woman we conned wasn't some sort of secret long-working urban legend madam that runs most of the girls all over New York City! You found the girl, she's home, she's safe, and that's all that matters! Do you know how many goddamn favors I had to pull so that you didn't end up in jail?" She started ticking off points on her hand. "You broke into a house with my guy, one of my guys that I work very hard to foster and put into jobs and places to help me out, and the two of you beat the shit out of how many people at a suspected brothel and drug house? No warrant, no cops? I almost fired Pedro for agreeing to your stupid plan, you playing him like that telling him about the girl, Jesus!

"Then you break into the place again after the police raid it and seal it off as a crime scene, and try to evade the patrolmen by leaping from a second-story window? Do you realize how insane this all sounds? Do you?" She looked out the window, clearly frustrated.

Ben slumped down. "I found a phone."

Kalli's head snapped back at him. "What?"

"I found a phone, hidden in the room. Her room. She had a phone, Kalli, the whole goddamn time." Kalli sat back, a stunned look spreading on her face. "Look, I know I fucked up, alright? You can fucking cool it with that," Ben continued, "But you know what that means, right? And think about it, think about just how an operation that the Sunnyside Madame might run would work if she-"

"Shut up," Kalli said, leaning forward. "Just, just shut up for five seconds. Pedro, turn around, head back to my office?"

"Yeah sure, no prob Miss K," the big man said, grinning.

.09

The afternoon was rainy and too warm really to be doing anything productive, but they were already dressed and ready to go, so she pulled her phone out and started dialing as the elevator doors to the apartment building opened. She knew a guy, a guy who could get them into a great club first later on that night, but first he'd take them out for food and maybe just hang out...

Ben, Kalli, and Pedro stood at the car in front of the building, the curb and front steps, normally bustling with people, young men sitting around waiting for nothing but knowing something's coming. Or the old lady

They were all gone, replaced with the white guy a beat-up jacket and messy hair that made him look like the clerk at the liquor store, too rumpled to ever get any real girl's attention. He looked sad, embarrassed almost. The other man, not white, older, could've been her dad, looked like one of her daddy's friends, but probably not. They all looked alike, see them whenever she'd run into him in the street in front of the store or the restaurant he worked at sometimes. This guy just looked stone-cold though, like he was disappointed. The white woman though? Dark hair, older than the one guy, in-between the two, in expensive shit, cut like a TV movie's version of a suit for a lady who was like, a secret agent or a lawyer.

"Maria, I think we need to talk." Kalli looked at the other girl, scared now at whoever it was that could scare off the usual crowd that populated the front steps of the building and the curbside. "Honey, I think you should just go home today."

.10

"You were right, that woman in the coffee shop's some big-time madam, manages 'like, a fucking ton' of houses and girls all over, Maria said. She was working for her, the money was good, and I guess when you're alone at school with not many friends, it's not that hard to turn on your classmates, peddle a good time, bring up an easy money and exciting time scenario.

"She ran away from home, nobody took her. She was working and living in that house like a home office or something, using the phone, hiding it so the junkies wouldn't find it and try to steal it to hock it for cash, tricking friends she'd make into getting hooked and then making them working girls."

"She's what, sixteen? Seventeen? Jesus," Kalli said, leaning back in her chair.

"Yeah, sixteen and already a sociopath."

"Oh, that's harsh, Ben. You gotta admit, it's pretty genius. Instead of getting some pretty older boyfriend to inevitably recruit these girls by becoming their boyfriend, instead start turning their friends? Girls'll trust another girl before any guy, even one they barely know. Especially teenagers." Kalli looked at the box like it was a pile of trash, curious but also disgustedly cautious. "What's this for?"

"Everything so far about the Sunnyside Madame I've been collecting since I first heard about her. I know we didn't really get anything from her and I haven't seen her around anymore since that time at the coffee shop, but-"

"She's gone to ground," Kalli interrupted, turning around the computer screen on her desk to face Ben. Tabs and windows of notes, pictures of the woman, and a map covered in red dots.

"Fancy, Mission Impossible-lady."

"Well, you piqued my interested. A single network of prostitution running in the five boroughs all managed by a single person in the end? Jesus Christ, this would be more insane and too-weird-to-be-true than the time the World Series was rigged."

"The World Series was rigged?" Ben said suddenly and incredulously. "Of course, didn't you know that?" Kalli said, tapping at the keyboard. "The Chicago White Sox against the Cincinnati Reds in 1919, big mob thing." Ben sat back down, a stunned look on his face. "Jesus, move on from that. That's not the point." Kalli moved the screen back, tapping at the keyboard as she did.

"So," Ben said, grinning, hands on the box, "What now?"

"Well, last sighting was in some place in Union Square, at that gross and overcrowded Taco Bell" Kalli stood up, fishing her cellphone and wallet from a desk drawer, heading for the office door. "Curious?"

"Let's go."

Black Ink

1.

———

THE COUPLE AT THE FAR end of the train care were going to break up.

Her body language and his, a stiff closeness, was a clear indicator of being used to being close to each other and still sitting like that out of habit, but her tightly-pursed mouth and his slumped-away shoulders? Totally going to break up, they're fighting now, so it'll probably be soon.

The old woman across from me? She's on her way to meet a "gentleman caller" or whatever it is older people my grandparents' age call it when they date. Her constant checking of her hair and makeup in the compact mirror and the nice outfit she was wearing in the middle of the day all screamed "lunch date."

No one else in the train warranted my attention or focus to play the game anymore, so I dug the printout from inside my coat pocket out, the directions and the emails between me and a Ms. Helen Ramnee at some book publisher in Manhattan that wanted to talk to me about a job. I had a few more stops to go before I'd disembark, and I re-scanned our correspondences, trying to pay attention to the emails so I could be prepared or something relatively close.

"Mr. Miles, we would like to discuss the possibility of hiring you for a job relating to…" I zoned out, jolted back to attention when the conductor's voice, scratchy and electronic, reminded me my stop was next, so I skimmed the rest of the email without really reading, looked at the address and name of the company, and stuffed the papers back into my jacket pocket. I had the time, they had a need, so I figured the $2.50 subway fare into Manhattan from Queens was worth it.

I got off as the doors hissed open and the few people riding the train this time of day got off with me, bundled up and faces down. Winter in New York City is probably my least-favorite season of the year, the cold always making my bad leg flare up.

Manta Books was a whole floor or two of a building a block from the Flatiron Building in Manhattan, a set of stars up to the third-floor door with "MP" and a stylized swoop, like a manta ray or a stingray or something, imprinted on the frosted-glass window. I knocked, and a young kid in a Batman t-shirt opened the door for me, then hustled past down the stairs, a box in his arms. Inside the office paper and books were stacked everywhere and I could see art tables, computers, an iPod plugged into some speakers by a coffeemaker playing something low and melodic. There were posters, some framed, some thumbtacked, up on the walls, and the low thrum of activity was constant. It was surprising to be honest, I always thought a book publisher was some staid old quiet office, not this, which reminded me more of the stint I did as a temp once at a newspaper, where everyone was wired on caffeine and constantly screaming at me about deadlines as I proofread papers shoved at me for two dollars a line.

"Mr. Miles?" A woman's voice, kind of authoritative but also casual, the kind that ran things in this kind of office with interns or assistants or gophers in Batman t-shirts, was at my left, and I found myself guided by the elbow over to the side against a far wall, a cubicle that was offering a little bit of privacy by a woman in blue hair and black-rimmed nerdy glasses. "Hi, I'm Helen Ramnee, pleasure to meet you. I'm the one that emailed you?" She sat down at the desk, motioning for me to sit in the chair opposite her, a diner chair loaded with books wrapped in plastic. "So, what do you know about Manta Books?" she asked as I tried to move the books off the chair to somewhere on the floor as surreptitiously as I could before sitting down.

"Honestly? Nothing," I admitted, sitting down to see action figures on Ramnee's desk staring at me. "We're a relatively small-to-medium-sized publishing imprint of Mega Comics," she said, and I looked around, realizing the posters all over the walls weren't book or movie posters, but comic book covers. "We do artbooks, reprints, collections, autobiographical stories..."

"Comic books, like biff-bang-pow?" I was never really a kid who read comic books, I'd always preferred other stuff, but I did know enough to know that they were big business these days.

She seemed a little irritated, but continued. "Not exactly, but at times, we have done superhero action books. This is our bread and butter, for the most part though." She handed me two books off of her desk, the top one a fat heavy hardcover, wide and long, the cover a black-and-white drawing of a sword with "Hawkblade Volume 3" in fancy calligraphy above it.

"Hey yeah, I know this." I flipped through the black-and-white pages of newspaper comic strips, some young prince warrior or whatever with a sword fighting knights and monsters. I vaguely remembered the name, my dad telling me that it was a classic or something on Sunday mornings at breakfast, but I never really paid attention.

"So?"

"So that is the classic newspaper comic strip 'Hawkblade,' by Kirby Hale," the other voice said as it approached me from out of my range of vision, the suit appearing to my right, smiling and sticking his hand out. "Steve Kane, Legacy Entertainment legal council."

"I asked Steve to come by during the meeting to represent our parent company, I hope you don't mind. Legacy are the principal shareholders of Mega Comics, and thus, us." Ramnee motioned to the second book she'd handed me, a smaller paperback, "Kirby Hale: American Comics." An older kindly-looking man at a drawing table holding a brush or a pen, in a full suit and tie, was on the cover, smiling. "That's Kirby Hale, the creator of 'Hawkblade.' Legacy and Manta Books has had the rights to reprint the entirety of comic for the past eleven years, and recently, we came into possession of the estate of Mr. Hale, who died in 1994."

"Okay?" I still wasn't entirely sure what it was they'd want from someone who mostly followed cheating husbands and wives or did bail bonds for guys swearing that this last arrests for meth was the last one, but I motioned like my grandfather did with one hand for him to go on, the way the old man did when I'd visit him and ramble on too long as a teenager. The lawyer and Ramnee were starting to look a little bashful, and I got the feeling that whatever it was, it was going to be something stupid and ridiculous.

"This sounds stupid and a little ridiculous, Mr. Miles," Kane said, "but when Mr. Hale died in 1994, it was somewhat sudden. The comic ran for two weeks after his death, during which the back stock of strips he'd turned in ran out. Then, it ended. The thing is…"

"Look, supposedly, Hale had one more comic to turn in, ready to go, but that was never published." The lawyer started to unload a few binders into my lap along with the books as she talked. "Manta Books and Mega Comics are working to bring 'Hawkblade' back, with new art and writing, and as part of that we're putting together the last volume of the reprints of the original collection." On top of the stack of stuff in my lap, the lawyer put a piece of paper and a pen. "Just sign here to get temporarily on payroll and get covered by our…"

"Wait, what am I signing? And what does any of this have to do with hiring me?" I batted his hands aside and shifted the stack onto already-overflowing desk.

"Mr. Miles, Manta, that is…we want you to find that last comic before the last reprint volume goes to print, before the reboot." Ramnee pointed to the piece of paper the lawyer gave me. "This temporarily puts you on Legacy's payroll, which allows you access to the Hale estate, where we believe the strip is, or at least some indication of where the strip is can be found."

"Hold up," I said, standing and taking a step back. If there was one thing I hated doing this job, ever since I stopped working for other agencies and doing it on my own, it was people overloading me with information about their oh-so-desperate cases all at once. "Let's slow down for a second. First off, what makes you think I could do this? I'm no comic book nerd."

"Look, we're in crunch mode, and just don't have the time and manpower to go through his stuff ourselves right now. To be honest, there's a lot of material, it's a full-time job. But don't worry, we'd actually like to pair you with Rob Wagner on this to help you. Rob's great, he'll be doing the new relaunch actually, he's a big 'Hawkblade' fan and researcher." Ramnee said, smiling. She touched one of the envelopes in the stack she and Kane gave me. "The keys to Hale's apartment here in the city, where he worked and where I understand most of the estate's things like papers and artwork ended up, are here."

"How long until you go to print or whatever?" I asked, as if I had some reservations still. It was a tempting offer, an easy job to help pad the bank account, and it couldn't be more than an hour or so's worth of work. Me and some nerd digging around for an afternoon in some boxes.

"The absolute limit before the last volume, which we'd like to include, has to go to the printers, is in a month and a half." Ramnee said, and I leaned over to look at the contract, see the daily pay rate, confirm my address, and I signed. "Not a problem, I'll find your comic book, easy."

"Strip. Comic strip."

"Right, whatever."

2.

"YOU GOTTA UNDERSTAND, 'Hawkblade' ran for fifty years almost non-stop, they only had a few repeats here and there for the holiday seasons and one stretch of reruns when Hale was in the hospital with appendicitis." Rob Wagner had shown up at my apartment, which doubled as my office, with more papers, more books, a computer covered in superhero stickers, and breakfast. It was the only reason I'd let him in at the inhumanly-early hour, but free coffee and fried egg sandwiches from the Greek guys at the stand down the block were impossible to resist, so the eyeglass- and "Hawkblade" t-shirt-wearing Rob Wagner, longtime fan and comic book writer and artist, was giving me a crash-course in newspaper comics and comic books, especially "Hawkblade." By now though the food was gone and the day was well into the afternoon, and I could feel my patience slowly wearing thin. Eagerness was never a trait I could really deal with.

"He had one of the most consistent runs as a newspaper cartoonist ever. Even when the boom hit in the Nineties with comics and then burst, even nowadays with newspapers dying off, they still rerun 'Hawkblade' strips, in print and online!" Rob, as I'd learned, had been a fan of the comic even before he was hired to rewrite and redraw it, doing a knockoff version on the Internet that drew the attention of Manta Books and the lawyer Steve Kane from Legacy, where they offered him a job that turned into the job of a lifetime for him. All of this had spilled out of him in the first hour he was over, alongside trivia about Batman, World War Two superhero and war comics, his professional-nanny girlfriend, and that he liked Italian food.

"What about 'Peanuts' and shit like that, that ran forever, didn't it?" My own limited knowledge of the funny pages was becoming painfully clear the more and more we talked, but Rob seemed to have no problem pouring out all sorts of information, occasionally showing me things on his laptop as I browsed the book on Hale that Ramnee gave me, reading his biography and the history of the comic, what tools he used, and other things I was pretty sure would ultimately be useless in helping with this case.

"Yes, it did, but the thing is that 'Peanuts' ultimately wasn't sequential storytelling. Every single strip is a complete joke and story all in one, you don't really have to read the one before to get the one in front of you.

"But 'Hawkblade,' it was different in that it was an ongoing adventure. I mean, look at the strips, they're just frozen moments in time!" He was getting into what I'd taken to calling, to myself of course, "nerd frenzies," showing me page after page from the collections we were looking at, some of which were from Rob's own collection, with various tabs and pencil notes in the margins. "Prince Valor and his father's trusted remaining aides guiding the young man on a hero's quest to gather allies and learn how to be an effective and wise ruler in order to retake the Kingdom of Talonor from from his evil uncle, the usurping King Rok? It's Campbell-esque in its simplicity but it works so well! No one does adventure strips anymore in comic books, let alone in newspapers or magazines. 'Hawkblade' was the go-to comic for young boys at the time, they even made a radio serial."

"So what're we looking for here?" I said, the books and papers piled up on the floor where Rob sat. I managed to maintain some dignity, perched on the edge of my desk, with egg stains and breadcrumbs down my shirt. "I just wanted you to get a good idea of the scope of this project, Ben," he said, digging into his bag for his laptop again. "I ran a 'Hawkblade' fan page on the Internet for years and even wrote about the comic for papers when I went to art school, I love this stuff. I did fancomics, I jumped at the chance when Manta asked me to helm this relaunch."

"I'm assuming this is a big deal with comic nerds."

"The biggest!" He stood up this time, showing me some news webpage with his face and a color stylized version of the main character, Valor, at the top. "Is that your art?" I said, surprised. It was drastically different from the flat black-and-white 2D strips, with bright colors and depth, like an oil painting I'd seen on a postcard.

"Yeah, that's from my art, the cover for the first issue." He closed the laptop. "My dad and I bonded over newspaper comics, especially 'Hawkblade,' when I was a kid. My old man used to want to be a writer, like Tolkien, but just never really got well-known for it or anything, so he loved that comic. I remember reading the reprints and reruns, getting the books with him, us both finding out about the 'legend of the lost strip.' I think that this would make the last volume of reprints perfect before I start the relaunch."

I had to admit, I was starting to get swayed over with Rob's enthusiasm. He and I couldn't be more than a few months, a year apart age-wise, but my own jaded burnout was easily-infected about finding this piece of paper in time. Also? It was a little fun, and made me feel as if I was somehow catching up on a childhood of missed opportunities reading Batman comics.

"Alright, how about we meet up tomorrow at the apartment," I said, sliding off the desk. At this point, as nice a guy as Rob was, I was starting to get sick of my apartment and of him. "We'll start seriously going through Hale's things, see what we can find there." Rob started to gather all his work up, shoveling the computer, books, and papers into his bag. "You think it'll be at his place? Supposedly, Hale's family never really went through his papers besides the will, just packed it all up. His sons all work in real estate and business now, so they weren't really art-types. I think they're both opening up a business using the money they got for the sale of the estate?" Rob stood as he put more papers in his bag, but they all tipped over and spilled out onto the floor. "Ahh, shit."

"Leave them, I'll just keep 'em here, might as well. Noon tomorrow? I have the key."

"OK, that works," he said, shouldering his bag and heading to the door. "See you then." I hear him take the stairs two at a time down to the street level, and then knelt to sweep all the loose photocopies of comics and pages from the Internet about Hale, plus Rob's own notes, up into my arms, dumping the pile of pictures and paper onto my desk. I picked up the top page, staring at it, a copy of one of the strips that Hale had done while the Korean War was going on, encouraging support of returning US troops "in the cartoonist's own words" instead of a regular comic. I remember Rob showing it to me earlier that day with great enthusiasum, but as I looked at it again, something struck me about how I could find out some more information about Kirby Hale.

He mentioned in the comic that he'd served in World War Two. That means the VA would have some sort of files on him. I swept up the copy of the page and stuffed it into my back pocket, picking up my phone and wallet and keys, heading out the door.

I might as well start somewhere.

3.

"COMIC BOOKS?" KALLI Kiliaris, my former boss and friend, asked me as she handed me a bottle of mineral water from the mini-fridge in her office and sat down at her desk, always the consummate professional compared to me. Kalli Kiliaris, far more successful as a bondsman and investigator, to the point that she had her own employees at the agency, was someone I went to for help when I didn't know how to start a case. These days she tended to do most of her work from in the office, so she'd always jump at the chance to help me out for some "actual" work.

"Well, newspaper comics, which the guy tells me is a totally different beast." I sipped the water, showed her the photocopy. "Anyway, despite the fact that I'm gonna be over there tomorrow going through his paperwork, I'm going to assume that what we're looking for isn't going to be there. Whoever went through the papers and rest of the estate must have at least looked around for some art, something to sell on the down-low?"

Kalli frowned, looking at the page and the line I'd underlined about Hale serving in the military. "Well, you would." Older than me by about a decade, every time I sat down with her it tended to evolve into one of those talks I always imagined younger siblings had with older sisters, in that she tended to treat me like an idiot. And to be fair, I was at times, and our history together was less than stellar when I was her employee. Still, we'd become better friends and work contacts since I'd struck out on my own, with her occasionally throwing a case my way from her stable of clients, usually weird stuff she knew her guys couldn't handle. This way, she could still jump in if it got interesting enough, knowing that I probably wouldn't ever say no to her. "So," she said, "what do you want to do?"

"Honestly, I want to find out some more about this guy. Like I said, me and the researcher'll be at Hale's place tomorrow but I know we won't find the art there, so anything else I can find out about him, like maybe old army buddies or something like that, anywhere he could have stashed some extra work?" I stood up, heading out the door.

"You think you'd maybe be able to do me a favor, look up military stuff or whatever on this guy?" Kalli was always infinitely better-equipped to do this sort of stuff, talk to people, cajole them, and convince them to just do her a little favor, just this once. I sucked at it, which is why I had to resort to asking her to do it for me. With my luck, I would more than likely either hit a brick wall, or get hit into a brick wall pissing some Army clerk off.

"Yeah, sure, no problem," she said dismissively, "I'll call you tomorrow when I get around to it."

"Thanks. I'll keep you in the loop, if you want?"

She laughed, "Oh yeah, real interested in, what is it again? 'Hawkwind'?" "Hawkblade," I said smirking, opening the door before almost bumping into her personal assistant, coming through the doorway with an armful of paperwork. "Sorry," she mumbled, passing by me and dumping the paperwork onto Kalli's desk with a noticeable THUMP. "Have fun with that," I said, letting myself out of the building and back onto the street in Astoria, out the door of the building that housed Kalli's offices alongside a real estate company on the ground floor and a cell phone repair place in the basement below street level. I turned the corner and headed down the street to my favorite Greek place for an early dinner, hoping that I'd beat the evening crowd.

I'd been reading the book about Kirby Hale on the train ride here from my place, thinking about what it was about the comic that had made it last so long or why it was so well-regarded. I honestly couldn't see the appeal of that sword-and-sorcery stuff, but whenever someone like Rob talked about it, you could tell it somehow was a good enough story to last all these years. What did strike me was how an Army guy like Hale, who was supposedly a bit of a recluse and as soon as he could, quit working in an office and worked out of his home and was reportedly quite the shy and quiet recluse, would have gotten along and made friends with the other cartoonists of the day. The book, as well as what Helen Ramnee and Rob had told me, indicated that for the most part the "gang" of cartoonists who were all published at the time in papers were riotous vets from the Lower East Side of Manhattan. There was even an anecdote about Hale involved in a fight between a group of American Nazi sympathizers and a gang of cartoonists led by "Johnny Flagg" creator Jack Lee. According to others, Hale was quite ferocious even though he had to be cajoled into coming with them from the floor the cartoonists' studio was down to the lobby. Sometime after that, he'd moved to a home studio.

Yianni's Kouzina, or Johnny's Kitchen, was packed by the time I got out there, and I could barely muscle through the growing crowd waiting for a table to get to Johnny's sister Koula at the front to ask about a table or even a seat at the counter. The wait was almost always astronomical, but the food would definitely be worth it. She saw me and nodded, reaching out through the crowd to grab my coatsleeve and guide me towards the kitchen.

I'd helped out Johnny and Koula a few years ago when they thought they were being shaken down about some mousaka recipe or something like that but had really been an old Greek mob vendetta gone wrong, as if those things ever go right. Since then I always managed to get, if not a table every time, then at least a little something extra when I showed up. Kalli had convinced me to help them out at a time when I wasn't really sure that I could handle something like that, and it really did sort of help make my name.

If nothing else, I got a chance to get a table at the most popular Greek place in Queens, and as Koula let me grab a seat at the staff table in the back corner of the kitchen with a bowl of hot lemon chicken soup, right-out-of-the-oven spinach pie, a pork chop, and peppers and a sausage doused in olive oil, I was reminded that that could be very, very satisfying.

4.

═══════════

I MET ROB OUTSIDE THE Lower East Side apartment building the next morning, thinking about whether or not Kalli had found anything, not to mention that I was pretty sure this was going to be a complete waste of time. Rob seemed unnaturally excited, though today it wasn't that infectious as last time. I was in work mode right now, and I knew that him fanboying all over the place was going to be supremely unhelpful.

I flipped through the keys the lawyer gave me as he hopped from foot to food with excitement. I could see he had a "Hawkblade" sweatshirt on under his coat and I rolled my eyes. "Ready?" I opened up the front door, we headed to the elevator, clicking the button. "I'm gonna be honest, I really don't think that we're going to find anything up there." I could see him sag a little big. "You never know. Schultz left his drawing table the exact same way after he did the last 'Peanuts' strip, it was that way when he died." Rob clicked the elevator button, peering up the open cage elevator shaft. "I think it's busted. Hoof it?"

It was on the third floor. My phone rang as we were at the front door, and I handed the keys to Rob as I answered. It was Kalli. "Look, I'm on the way to a meeting but my assistant just brought me something you might find interesting. There was no Kirby Hale in the U.S. Military. Not Army, Air Force, the Marines, Navy, not even the freaking National Guard or the Coast Guard or the police. I thought you said he was some kind of military hero?"

"Yeah, I know. Hold on," Inside, Robb was standing in the middle of the old living room, touching things, looking at the dusty photos on the walls. "Are you sure that Hale was in the Army?"

He put down the stack of books he'd found on the coffee table, the imprint of where it'd been left still visible. "Yeah, it was one of the big selling points of the strip, an Army veteran who fought for his country? He never talked about it and hated when other people did, but supposedly the fact that he was modest about it was well-liked. Strip sales guys never shut up about it."

"I'll call you later, I said into the phone, hanging up. I picked up a stack of mail in the front room off the table, slipping it into my bag to look at later. "Anyway, I'd hoped that his old army buddy contacts might lead us somewhere, but now I don't know."

"Well, if you think about, this isn't a huge deal. After all, Stan Lee was Stanley Lieber, Jack Kirby was Jacob Kurtzberg, Hal Foster was Harold, they all changed their names or shortened them."

"Who the shit are those people?"

He shook his head. "Never mind. The point is, all we need to do is find something with his real name on it, right? Isn't that what PI's like you do, track down real names, do stakeouts, stuff like that?"

I started flicking lights on and off, realizing that the shaded windows were keeping the whole apartment in perpetual darkness. No power was in the place, so we started to open the windows, drawing blinds and raising the shutters, letting late-morning sunlight filter in and make the old empty apartment a little less gloomy and foreboding. "You watch too many movies. Or comic books. Look, unless I can find something besides some mail, like a diploma or a lease, then we're just gonna be spinning our wheels when it comes to his original name. If he legally changed it, then that's different, there should be a record somewhere hopefully, a lawyer's office. I can check around some more. So what happened that his kids aren't cashing in on all this crap? Why keep it like this?"

Rob poked his head into what looked like a spare bedroom full of trash bags, and I followed in to start ripping the rotting old plastic open to spill old shirts and slacks everywhere. Clearly a donation to the Salvation Army never went through. "I just know that they sold the apartment and contents recently after hanging onto it for the sake of keeping the apartment off the market. This is a desirable neighborhood, my ex lived down near here and her rent was nausea-inducing. I heard he was pretty adamant about his kids not getting into comics, they're probably gonna flip this whole building with the estate sale money. New York City real estate."

"Ahhh." The fashionable area was crawling with young couples, coffee shops, the type of gentrification that would normally have zoned in on the small hidden old walkup if not for the battered front door and stairs, the windows on the street level barred and shuttered.

I left the room as Rob was rifling through the closets, poked my head into one of the apartment's dark rooms, finding what I assumed was the studio. I dug up the tiny throwaway flashlight I always carried around, a freebie from a bail bonds convention I went to last year, letting the weak light flicker around the room. There was a chair by a drawing table next to the room's single shuttered window, and all around there were boxes and boxes of what I assumed were paper. "Hey, I found his studio."

Rob was barely in the room before the contents of one of the boxes were in his hands, rifling through them. "Well?" I asked, kneeling down next to him to start rifling through another one. "This is amazing, it's all sketched, thumbnails, this is awesome stuff!" He started handing me what I realized was scrap paper, stuff in faded pencils, smears of inks from what I figured were brushes and pens on the borders. "What is this? Scrap?"

"What? No, this is amazing. Some collectors are paying top-dollar for this stuff. Thumbnails from a Gray 'Little Orphan Annie' strip were auctioned off by American Heritage for like five grand last year." He was stacking paper as he took it out of the boxes, moving twice as fast as me. "I still keep comics in longboxes," he said, answering my unspoken question. "So far though, none of this looks like a finished strip."

"What's the last strip supposed to be, anyway?" I asked. We'd been spending so much time talking about Hale that I realized I didn't even know exactly what it was I was going to be looking for. "Well," Rob said, settling in, "the last strip that was published had Prince Valor and his aides looking to establish defense posts around their castle, because the invading..." I held up a hand, sighing. "Alright, I get it, so the missing one's a follow up to that? What, the attack?"

"Well, that's the assumption. Or it's more planning shown. Hale was a long-form storytelling and by that point he pretty much had free reign with how long he took to reach the conclusion of a storyarc, he was Schultz-level of..."

"Alright, I get it." Rob Wagner was smart but, I was realizing, had an annoying tendency to trail off easily. After a few hours, it was pretty much a foregone conclusion that it wasn't in the apartment. In fact just about everything we'd seen was penciled drawings on paper, or pages from notebooks.

We were in that apartment for almost two hours, rooting through boxes, shaking out books, going through everything and anything. No completed strips, barely anything concretely "Hawkblade"-related.

"Look, the strip's not here. You find any actual complete art?" I'd gotten a look at what a Hale strip looked like as an original, so at least I vaguely knew what to look for size- and shape-wise, and nothing we'd come across was even close. "No, a lot of thumbnails and pre-production art, but not the strip." He looked a little dejected. "Are we gonna be able to find this before we head to print with the last volume?"

"Hell, I don't know, why don't you guys use some of this crap?" I waved my arms around. "There's gotta be at least three or four books' worth of stuff, right? I saw those volumes at the office, it'd work, right?"

He took a few sheets from one box, carefully sliding them into the empty plastic sleeves of the binder, putting the binder back into his bag. "I guess," he said. "I'm gonna take some of these into the office with me, I still have a script to work on." I'd forgotten that Rob was supposed to be writing the comic as well, attached to me because of his prodigious knowledge of the comic. "Hey," I said, feeling bad at his lack of excitement, the way a parent patronizes a hurt or embarrassed child, "You got any of the comic you could show me?" I was starting to feel embarrassed at how bad I felt that he was so down. "Really?" he said, looking up. "Yeah sure, email me something," I said, heading toward the apartment door. "Come on, let's go, I gotta go do some things."

We left the apartment building and parted ways on the sidewalk, Rob going back to the Manta offices to use their studio space, apparently a part of the upper floor I hadn't seen, while I was intent on heading home after stopping off for some Chinese food. I was honestly not that surprised that we didn't find the strip there, especially after what I'd read about Hale in the book that they'd given me.

The author of the book quoted a little too much from a 1980 interview with him in some comic book trade magazine or journal, and one point had stuck with me about how Hale said that he considered it a trade as much as an art, and refused to "dilly-dally."

I had to admit it was a quote that made me respect the man, sitting in that apartment all day churning out work, a one-man assembly line of funnypage material. But if he was that prolific, then that meant that he would have finished the strip entirely before letting someone know that it was done.

Hopefully the stack of mail that I'd grabbed would maybe lead to something. Technically, it could be considered mail theft or mail fraud, but since I was working for the new owners of the estate, I figured I was covered. Just in case a random cop stopped me on the walk home, asked why I had a messenger bag full of mail from an apartment on the Lower East Side on me.

If it hadn't been found immediately after his death, that meant that it'd been finished a while but held back, obviously. But why? That didn't make any sense. The only thing I could think of was that the strip had been finished, was literally on the table ready to go, but at the last minute moved or taken.

That night I dreamed about a young prince in a weird bowl cut and tunic and pantyhose with a glowing sword, and I woke up in a start, rolling off the bed with a resounding and painful "THUMP" on the hardwood floors.

I was starting to hate comic books.

5.

———

"NO, WOULDN'T WORK."

"What, why?" I was on the phone with the Ramnee woman the next day, talking about what we found at the apartment. I floated the idea I'd talked to him by her about using the spare art instead of the missing strip.

She paused on the other end of the phone, and I could hear alongside the static the faint hum of the office's hustle and bustle. Finally she answered, a low almost-whispering tone that sounded like she didn't want to be heard and saw someone talk like this in a spy movie. "Because we already solicited it with the missing strip."

"You what? Solicited?"

"Yes, it means we advertised to distributors and bookstores already. We...we might have already told the printers that we had the strip and it would be part of the volume's manuscript. Everyone assumed it'd be in the estate's various holdings, but now that you've gone through the apartment, we know that it's really missing. That's why we brought you in, just in case. That's why I gave you the absolute deadline."

I hung my head, massaging my eyes. The day had barely started for me and I already was tired and had a headache, not to mention that the day-old Chinese I'd eaten for dinner last night after getting back from Hale's old apartment and making some calls was not sitting well. "So basically, we're a little screwed if I can't find it."

"Definitely. Nothing major here with the bosses per se, all those sketches you and Rob found could definitely be used, but in the public eye, we'd be kind of fucked, and we're still a small enough publisher that that negative press could kill who knows how many future projects."

"Alright." I peered at the pile of mail I'd taken and a list that Kalli Kiliaris had sent me, "Look, I've got a could of maybe-leads, trying to track down any old second homes or friends that could be holding on to some of Hale's stuff, and if that's the case, they could have the strip. I'll keep you updated and meet with Rob tomorrow."

We hung up, and I got to work.

Like I'd told Rob, everyone always thinks that private eye work is mostly stakeouts full of bad coffee, late nights following sleazy characters, or laying it on thick to break a witness when the cops can't. The truth? It's a lot of fucking phone calls, reading, and sitting around hoping someone returns your emails and voicemails. The only stakeouts I ever did were intensely tedious and made me feel like a scumbag watching some unhappy wife cheating on her awful husband, or getting bored making sure a bond investment didn't skip town after his bail was made. Going through the mail was, in comparison, a welcome walk in the park. Most of it was the usual stuff widowers over a certain age would have gotten back then before he died, solicitations for charity donations, bills, junk condo crap, mostly nonsense.

I sorted the bills from the junk, then popped open the cheap lockblade knife I got in Chinatown and used as a letter opener, going through all of them. Even paid bills and receipts could end up being useful at times, or at least that's what Kalli had said to me once when I'd thrown out a ton of mail after checking an apartment for a case for her by accident. I ended up elbow-deep in the trash, finding ripped envelopes mixed with old Thai and Mexican food and bathroom trash to look up where a credit card had been used the month before.

Sometimes you learn the hard way.

For the most part, it was all uneventful. Bills paid by check, in full, all the time, the only late unpaid ones the ones he got after he died. The last two in the pile though made me pause for a second, a wrong name on the right address. A former resident? But Hale had lived in this apartment for years, according to the paperwork he'd seen from the estate, so this "B. C. Mello" was...a development. Isn't that what a real private eye would say?

Something was bothering me as I opened up both bills, one for a P.O. box and another from a bank for a safety-deposit box, the second one even more confusing. The bill was for the monthly payments on a box under the name of Kirby Hale, but in the care of the B. C. Mello name. Suddenly I sorted through more junk mail, finding one, two, three pieces of solicitations for condos, and there it was;

Another was for the name B. C. Mello.

I fumbled around for my cellphone, thumbing the glass touchscreen to get it dialing for Kalli. Her voicemail beeped after the digital voice said her name. "Hey, I need you to run another name for me through the military thing, if you can. B. C. Mello, B and C being initials, Mello with two L's and one O. Thanks."

I'd looked up all the names that Wagner had said to me earlier, cartoonists who'd changed their names, and for the most part, the changes from birth name to print name were pretty much just simplifications, some basically turning Jewish and Jewish-sounding names in WASP-y names. This was a pretty drastic change, but still, nothing that new.

I was curious why he'd have a P.O. box and a safety deposit box, though I'm sure there were some of Mom's pearls or maybe World War 2 bonds in that. Maybe remnants from a mistress? Some place to get fan mail? Still, it was something, a lead I could definitely use. I dialed the phone again, and Rob answered. "Hello?"

"Hey, I think I might have something. Does the name Mello mean anything to you about Hale? A friend, his real name, another cartoonist?" I went over to the fridge, digging around for something to eat as I heard Rob on the other end of the phone scrambling around. I realized he was probably at his art desk or whatever drawing guys with swords fighting other guys with swords, and I felt a pang of remorse keeping him from actual work. Still, Ramnee had him working with me to find this strip, so I shook it off and treated him the way anyone would treat a research assistant, like a paid slave. He could be a hotshot comic book artist some other time.

"No, why?"

"Just a hunch. You sure? Not his wife's maiden name or anything like that? His kid's wives maiden names?"

"Why would I know that?"

"You're the Kirby Hale fanclub president, why wouldn't you?"

He sighed on the other end of the line. "I can look it up if you want, I have a bunch of mail I got sent and CC'ed on when the deal to get the rights to the title happened, there's all sorts of family names in there."

"Perfect." I hung up and went back to the desk with the leftover Thai I'd discovered just as the cellphone rang again, Kalli calling me back.

"You know, I should probably start charging you."

"What, like a client?"

"No, like an idiot fee." I could hear the office in the background, paper rustling, people busy. Kalli usually kept her office quiet even on busy days, I remember the battles to try to get in to see her about something but she was maintaining a strict line between the Outside Office and the Inside Office, and I couldn't go into the Inside Office until things had quieted down. She claimed it helped her work, and after a certain point, I stopped caring as long as my paychecks got signed.

"Hey what's going on over there?"

"That's what I wanted to talk to you about, dummy. Do you not remember? I had you and Darryl Hathwin and that other girl, with the blue mohawk, whatshername, working on the filings for this for months. The Caramello thing? The mobster from the 40's?"

"Vaguely?" I was starting to get an odd feeling, one that was screaming You Are So Out Of Your League.

"The enforcer for the Maribelli family in the 30's and 40's? Are you kidding me? It was the first thing you worked on for me, it's why I hired you, to help sort through all the paperwork when the FBI declassified all that shit and let my office have it back finally." I could hear the exhasperation through the phone. "Look, I'm sending some stuff over by courier, and as of right now, as your friend and far more competent worker, I'm on this with you. This involves us whether you want it or not. I have to go." Kalli hung up, leaving me standing there with the phone by my desk with the cold takeout container.

Holy shit.

Kirby Hale was Bobby Caramello.

6.

<hr>

"JESUS."

"That's what I said."

The lawyer, Kane, stood up with his back to us, me and the Ramnee woman sitting at his desk. I'd brought the Caramello news to her, and she had dragged me and the sheaf of papers I'd brought from Kalli into a cab to the lawyer's office, furiously tapping at her phone the entire ride.

"Alright, who knows this?" he said, turning around.

"I do, my ex-boss, you two. I haven't told Rob yet."

"Don't," Ramnee said, "he's got enough on his plate as it is, working with you and wrapping up the first few issues of the relaunch. This...this is not good. This whole thing could blow up in our faces."

"I'm a little confused still as to who Mr. Hale really was," Kane said, "You said he was involved in some bank robbery?"

I looked through the packet that Kalli had sent me. "To put it mildly, yeah. Robert 'Bobby' Caramello. Born in Chicago in 1919, went to work for the Maribelli Family in 1930, a string of arrests for strongarming, bank robbery, extortion, only a few minor convictions, claimed he was a 'suit salesman' or a 'dressmaker.' The usual stuff when it comes to mob guys back then.

"He was on a job at the 1943 U.S. First National robbery, a shit-ton of gold in crates. Caramello, according to FBI and police reports, actually served in the US Army, '41 to '42, a stint in Europe. Thanksgiving day, 1943, Caramello and the gold are all gone, no trace of either. Caramello, who according to the cops used the pseudonym 'C. B. Mello' or 'B. Mello', had basically disappeared off the face of the earth. The gold, which the police had a bit of a trail on, was gone too. No one knows what happened to either." The gold was a bit of East Coast law enforcement urban legend, with leads periodically surfacing once in a while. When her dad had been running the agency, Kalli Kiliaris had even taken a pass on it as a favor for the FBI briefly. That's where I had come in, but that was another story for another day.

"'Hawkblade' debuted January 1944, but it had been picked up months earlier," Ramnee said, "So he'd been pitching under the Hale name for a while." Ramnee flipped through her phone. "Rob sent me all the stuff you two have found so far, as well as his own research from before you were hired. According to one of the few interviews he gave, Hale, or Caramello or whatever his name was, said he'd been trying to pitch strips since 1935. How would no one notice? What actual proof is there here?"

"There's one promotional photo of Hale the syndicate had for years. I looked at it and he doesn't look a thing like the mugshots of Caramello," Ramnee handed me her phone, the side-by-side pictures showing two very different-looking me. One was an early mugshot and clearly a younger man, rough-looking with curly hair and a smooth face. The other was heavier, with a moustache, glasses, different haircut, bowed down over a drawing board. She was right, the two looked completely different. The Hale picture was barely even a profile, it'd be impossible to tell. And if he'd changed his voice or posture, used an accent or spoke deeper or lisped? Who'd know? "It was the 30's, no one had Google or background checks of any sort. He said he was a veteran and had worked as a dressmaker before getting picked up," she continued.

"A dressmaker? What Caramello said he did?"

"Yeah, though to be honest that doesn't mean much. You know, suits, shirts, fancy dresses. Most mobsters had front jobs out of sham businesses in that era. Mickey Cohen in LA was famous for having an expensive suit and had boutique."

"That's it?"

"Well the B. C. Mello and C. Mello name we found all over Hale's mail at his apartment matches up to the alias Caramello used to rent apartments and safety-deposit boxes around New York City. The first time he got picked up, the police reports said he gave his name as Bob Christopher Mello. B. C. Mello."

"So nothing too definite," Kane said.

"No, but it's too much of a coincidence for it to not make sense. The timeline matches up, the alias being used by Hale for some mail, I mean one or two accidental fuck-ups by the Post Office, but Rob found a ton of receipts and old mail under the Mello name in the papers we got from the Hale apartment. It has to be him," I said.

"Why would he use an old alias like that if he was trying to hide from the mob?" Helen said, "wouldn't they know to look for it?"

"Who knows." I was getting fidgety, hoping to get out of here and get back to work as soon as possible, get this over with. The fact that this stupid comic strip had already turned out to not be where everyone said it would be was enough of an annoyance, and making me feel like I was stuck in the cheap paperback spy books that everyone thought my job was like.

"The syndicate had a known and wanted gangster as a nationally-known cartoonist? No wonder he never wanted to meet with anyone, Jesus." Kane was saying over and over. He sat down, looked at Ramnee, who shrugged. I got the distinct and unpleasant feeling I was about to get suckered into something. Either that, or there was some sort of weird pre-agreed upon crap going on between the two.

Turns out I was right. Or wrong. Both, neither...you know what I mean.

"Mr. Miles, we're willing to increase your fee to keep going. We understand that this seems like it'd be complicating issues, but the fact of the matter is that the 'Hawkblade' reprints are big money..."

"And you wanna protect big money," I finished. "Look, I'm not gonna lie that this seems sorta weird, and I'm sure in a couple of years when Rob or you guys do another book on this guy you'll be including this interesting tidbit in there as well. I know I would. But honestly, I'm only hesitant because the US First National gold thing's an urban legend for a reason. Hale or whatever his name is probably either fenced it himself, lost it, or never did steal it from the bank.

"My ex-boss and her agency said they'd help me, she's got a bit of history with this case. The pricetag's new number is gonna be a bit more than just my fee."

"That's fine," he said, picking up the phone. "We'll be in touch with her firm and get a corporate account set up. I'm assuming you'll still be working with Rob?" At this point you could assume I was going to put on a cape and fly out the window too Holy-Fuck-What-Land, and it wouldn't be too far off from the truth. Stuff was going too fast too soon, and I didn't like it.

"Yeah sure, whatever."

The Ramnee woman, who had buried herself in her phone again the instant Kane started talking, got up suddenly. "If the focus is going to be on the reprint, we might have to push a few issues of the new thing back, especially if you're gonna need Rob full-time on this to make the deadline." She walked out, leaving me behind with Kane.

"You'll have to excuse her. Unless you're in the know you wouldn't know, but well, we're trying to line up a 'Hawkblade' movie so having the books ready to go and in the marketplace before the news is official is a big thing."

I got up to leave. "Look, with Kalli Kiliaris my workload's cut significantly on this, we'll have the strip soon, pretty sure. The only thing I'd be worried about is word of this getting out, having to deal with urban legend treasure-hunter types." I'd run into them before, big on hiring guys like me to lead them around. It'd died out after the Geraldo thing in the 80's but when I'd first started working for Kalli they'd come in a lot, wanting "professional consulting" services to help them blowtorch a basement safe open in a house that they'd basically broken into on the Lower East Side or in Staten Island.

"You're not worried about, you know, mobsters?" the lawyer practically whispered, and I had to fight to keep from laughing in his face.

"What, Caramello's old crew? They're probably all dead or they took the gold from him, and he's dead already, why would they care? I'm telling you, this will get annoying, I'm sure someone will bother me, but it won't be anyone as dangerous as a mob hitman, probably just more fucking Internet nerds digging around."

Out on the street, I looked around, trying to figure out exactly where the hell I was. The car ride over with Helen had thrown me off, and I had to admit, my inner map and compass weren't the greatest. I found a subway station that would, eventually, get me home, and descended underground.

I was starting to hate comics.

7.

———————

"OKAY, THANKS." I HUNG up the phone, threw the notepad back onto the desk, and put my head down on the wood surface next to it. Trying to track down any level of activity regarding the Mello or Hale names around the old apartment or in general was turning out to be almost impossible. Checks from a third party paid the rent on Hale's apartment for years from a bank that didn't exist anymore, and after that it'd been wire transfers, and no one was going to be sharing private banking information with me without something like a court warrant or whatever. The various owners of the building, at least the ones that were alive still, had no clue what I was talking about when I finally got in touch with them, or who Kirby Hale was.

Rob had been silent for a few days, so I walked over to the fridge while on my phone. "Yeah?" he muttered after a few rings, sounding distracted.

"Any luck on your end?" I found a frozen Weight Watchers meal, a leftover from an old girlfriend, and proceeded to try and rip it open to put in the microwave with one hand while holding the phone.

"Not really, though I'm actually heading out of here for a work thing soon that might help. You see the email I sent you?"

"You send me email?"

"Yeah I've sent you a bunch, Helen gave it to me," I heard faintly, like he'd put the phone down and was yelling at it from a few feet away. "I'm giving a talk at a museum in Ohio about comic books for some librarians, and they might have a few things there about Hale or Mello or whoever, I think. Look," the voice got normal again, the phone picked up, "I'm out the door for a few days, but check it out. Gotta go!"

The microwave beeped as he hung up, and I stared at the kitchen counter for a second. I'd put the turn-up remnants of the frozen meal down next to the pile of mail I'd taken from Hale's apartment, forgotten after the whole realization of Hale being Caramello. I scattered the pile on the counter, the bills and junk that I'd discarded and ignored, staring at the names and addresses.

The NOT AT THIS ADDRESS sticker was barely sticking out, the obnoxious orange of the label the Post Office used the only thing that made it stand out amongst the pale white of envelopes and ugly beige of my countertop.

I pulled the envelope out of the pile, the rest of the mail scattering onto the counter and down to the floor as I walked back to my desk, grabbing at my pocket knife and slitting the envelope open to pull the letter out, stiff with age and something else, moisture. The envelope, I realized, was hard and crinkly. It'd been caught in the rain before being brought inside, and a part of my brain started to think to when the last time it rained long enough for mail to get trapped outside and soaked.

It was from an alarm company, reminding whoever lived at the previous address that the payment for a system installed in an apartment listed below had been disconnected due to a lack of payment. The date was a few weeks ago, right when I remembered the big rainstorm had hit us.

The address was in the middle of nowhere in the Bronx, past the furthest the subway even went. I'd been there once or twice, enough to know where it was, not enough to have any kind of connections or idea of what to expect.

Still, t was something, and at this point I needed something to happen. The deadline was starting to approach and I was feeling a little bad that I'd spent two days doing nothing but hoping someone smarter than me would call with a clue or a tip, while I read all the comics that Rob had left for me at my place and ate pizza while avoiding Ramnee's phone calls.

I reached for my phone, swiping for Kalli's number as I was out the door, down the stairs, the front door slamming closed behind me. "Hey, you need to meet me in the Bronx."

"Uh huh, sure." I could hear paper shuffling in the background. "Look, you and I both know that this comic thing is dying out. The kid sent me that email, and while it might pan out with something, Caramello's going back to being another thing just left to...wait, why exactly are you asking me to come to the Bronx?" She was excited now and the shuffling of paper had stopped, whatever she was doing put down as I was out the building door and on the street, grabbing a free paper, looking for a bus stop. "What do you have?"

I smiled.

8.

BY THE TIME I GOT TO the apartment it was dark already. I'm sure stopping to get something to eat and then answer text messages from an on-and-off girlfriend really didn't help, but Kalli had told me she was running behind coming to meet me there anyway, so I figured I could afford to dilly-dally around.

It was a piece of paper we were after, it's not like it could up and run away, I told myself.

At the front of the building, a shithole of a place that didn't even have the odd comforting familiarity of young teenagers hanging out around the stairs or the lobby, I stood around for a bit, checking my phone to see if anything came in from Kalli.

"Hey, man!" I heard a voice yell, a ways away from me, and I turned towards it.

The first rule of people trying to get your attention in New York City, especially in places that are dumps, is never respond. Especially if the person is relatively close to you and uses "man," "buddy," or "bro." All they want is to get close enough to you to try to strongarm you. From further away though? Totally fine.

At least, that's what I thought as I turned to the voice, my instincts somehow overriding common sense. The hit came from behind me, not in front of me, the second guy's voice just a "hfff" of exhertion from punching me in the back of the head and then shoulder-checking me to make sure I stay down on the ground. His shadow made the space over me darker, blocking out the ambient nighttime light of streetlights, windows, and I heard the first voice, again from further away.

"Watch him," it hollered, and I tried to look up, seeing someone, young, white, in snappy "business casual" trying desperately to stuff a rag into a can of gasoline, standing under one of the windows of the front of the big old building. The DUM DUM of pressure on the can was somewhat humorous, watching this guy try to get the can over his head without the soaked rag brushing against his head. Whoever Tweedledee and Tweedledum were, I'm assuming they were going for some kind of Molotov cocktail-effect on the first floor. Of course, I thought, it'd help if they lit the rag up first before throwing the non-breakable metal can into the window of the first floor apartment.

The barred window, I realized.

The guy standing over me nudged me with a knee. "Hey, eyes down asshole. Hurry up!" he yelled.

"Relax!" the other guy said, realizing his mistake. So much for that much luck in my favor. He held the can aloft with one hand, the other poking around his pants pocket for a lighter or something. Briefly, I realized that if they did manage to set the first floor of this apartment building on fire, two things could happen.

One possible outcome involved the entire building going up in flames. But, as I thought about it, on all fours on the sidewalk, the likelyhood of that happening was nil.

Why the hell would anyone want to set this old dump on fire? If the outside denizens of the street and stoop had been chased off, it'd explain where everyone was, though again, this brought me back to why the hell anyone wanted to burn this building down. Unless of course...

No. No goddamn way. No way in hell that this had anything to do with that stupid comic. I shook my head there on the sidewalk. "No fucking way," I muttered as the guy over me kicked me in the side, though the force wasn't really that much.

"What the fuck is going on?" I heard a familiar voice yell suddenly from down the block. The tap-tap-tap of sensible business bootlike shoes, Kalli Kiliaris's footwear walking and then running at us. "Ben?"

"Back up, lady," I heard the one with the gas can say as he struggled, "Just back off, nobody gets hurt."

Oh Jesus.

"You stupid piece of shit!" she said, swinging one arm suddenly. The asp snapped hard on his one arm, buckling it. Ten inches of metal and plastic hurt like hell, I remember her jokingly using it around the office when I worked for her.

I never even saw her take her hand out of her pocket.

"Holy shit!" he yelled, the gas can tumbling out of his grip, dripping and banging against his head, the smell of fuel everywhere. The thin metal container and rag smashed on the sidewalk as he turned to try to run after his friend, the arm Kalli smashed with the 10-inch collapsible baton dangling at his side. "Wait the fuck up!"

"Goddamn idiots," she muttered. "Sorry, I drove up, finding parking was hell. What the hell was that?"

"No clue."

My phone buzzed as we stood there, and I read the text from Wagner, scrolling through it a few times and rolling it over in my brain. Huh.

"Never mind, maybe I do."

9.

———

THE COPS TOOK THEIR sweet time picking up Mr. I-Don't-Know and Mr. Where's-My-Lawyer while we sat there, Kalli doing most of the talking while I hung back and texted with Wagner furiously, trying to look like someone with a real job that a cop wouldn't want to actually deal with.

"Come on," Kalli said, waving me down the block, "they're not going to let us in tonight, so let's get something to eat and come back later. A car's gonna sit on the spot here in case someone tries something."

I didn't feel good leaving the apartment, even for another few hours, so I called Helen Ramnee as we strolled, let her know that there was definitely a lead or two going on that would lead us to, if not the comic, then at least some juicy details for her to put in the book. It seemed to help her un-frazzle, which made me feel a little bit productive as we strolled up to a no-name diner a few blocks away. "I saw this place as I parked," Kalli said noncommittally, walking in and, like every other place in New York, started talking Greek to the old man at the counter. A big fat grin split his face as he responded, and I rolled my eyes.

My former boss and big-shot PI company owner still couldn't help showing off that she used to be a Greek girl from Queens working in a diner through high school, hoping one day to, at the very least, not end up with four ungrateful kids and a church schedule to rival March Madness. Every diner in New York, she'd tell me periodically, was either owned or run by Greeks, and it almost always worked out for her. A few bucks off the tab, an extra slice of pie, something like that.

Of course, it also still helped her cultivate one of the best information networks in New York City, because who knows more than a nosy diner cook who overhears every cop and late-night weirdo at the counter talking about work?

"So what makes you think that it's in there?" she asked as we sat down, the same slightly-dingy plastic drinking glasses of water and ice in front of us that you find in every diner in New York, a smiling older man bringing us coffee cups. Kalli and him exchanged some words in Greek before she looked back at me, putting the now-collapsed asp and her cell phone on the table by the sugar and salt-n-pepper shakers.

I rubbed the back of my head. Those kids might have been punks, but the one had definitely thought far too long and hard about punching someone in the back of the head, because I was still a little dizzy. "Who knows. At this point, it's the only lead I've got, and honestly I feel a little bad that it's taken so long to get anything besides a faint tie-in to some weird old organized crime urban legend."

The coffee was awful, even with the four spoonfuls of sugar I poured into it, but the harsh dark burn of it helped ease the throbbing in my head and steady my breathing as my side recovered a bit. "I mean Jesus Christ, I was looking for a piece of paper, I got all this cash from these people and I got almost nothing out of it. They'll get even less if I don't find something."

She didn't say anything, checking her phone as I talked. "What was that text you got before?"

"Hmm? Oh that, the guy I'm working with, said he found some weird clue or whatever. He says it's tied into the whole mob thing, so I guess we'll see whatever it is when he gets back tomorrow." I scrolled through my phone. "Something about the 'Hawkblade' fan club and fan prizes with clues? He's a terrible texter, I can't really tell. It can wait." I pushed away from the booth. "Whatever, I think I just want to go home at this point, the apartment can wait."

Kalli shook her head. "Fuck no, Ben. Are you kidding me, after getting me to come all the way down here and then probably break that stupid wannabe-gangster's arm?" She stood up too, tossing a few dollar bills down on the table.

"Let's go see what's inside."

***

10.

***

"FOUND IT."

"Wait, what?"

The cops were gone, clearly having decided after a while that it wasn't worth it to maintain a presence after after all. We'd circled the block a few times in her car to make sure no cop car actually had been left behind in some misplaced sense of duty, Kalli and I got into the lobby of the building, a dingy old apartment building that still had enough decrepit pre-war decor going on to almost seem like a forgotten era-sorta place, the kind of building you'd think would be part of a mysterious cult or some kind of haunting.

It wasn't thought, it was just another old building forgotten by time and by just about everyone except the tenants, who probably paid next to nothing for rent, holding out generation to generation until the last of them died off or moved away, letting this get turned into some kind of three-thousand-a-month condominium with a doorman. It didn't feel that far off in the lobby, but for a moment, it still hadn't happened.

I'd dug the piece of mail I'd managed to keep in my pocket this whole time out, looking for the apartment number. Dutifully trudging up to the door, the corner apartment door yielded to the mechanical skeleton key Kalli fished out of her coat pocket, what looked like an electric toothbrush had sex with a power drill and sounded almost as loud. The apartment was, unlike the other one, the complete opposite, with simple neat furniture, a few books, a TV, an unused kitchenette, and a bedroom with a closet full of moldy old clothes. There was a layer of dust on almost everything, and the power was clearly out. Unlike the mess in the Hale apartment, this felt almost minimalist, less a home than a hotel room. I'd swiped the flashlight on my phone awake, while Kalli clicked a small light from her pocket on. In the dark, we looked through cabinets, mostly-empty bookshelves, and under pillows, and wherever we could. At one point, I opened the closed curtains, the ambient outside light of the night came through to help a little, though, I admitted to myself, we were still rooting through a strange dark apartment that had been closed up for years in the middle of the night.

We'd been in there for just a short while, maybe twenty minutes before Kalli came across the strip. After all this, I wasn't even the one who found it, hidden in a book on baseball under the TV, in a clear plastic envelope between two pieces of tracing paper.

"Well, that was...easy?" I ran my flashlight beam over it, black ink and, still visible, a few jots and dashes of pencil and white paint or corrective fluid on the paper, still mostly white after all these years. "Here," Kalli handed it to me, "I'm gonna have some of my guys come over here, you should take that." She put her flashlight away and fished a cellphone out instead, dialing.

"Why?" I didn't quite know how to hold the whole thing, which felt stupid to just have in my hands but wasn't rigid enough to put under my arm. Kalli ignored me, "Hey, it's me. Look, see if you can call Alphonso and maybe Rich...they just got back? Good, put Rich on. Hey," she turned away from me, talking. Alphonso and Rich, I vaguely remembered from when I worked there, were two of the older employees, an ex-cop and a former ambulance driver. She walked out the still-open door and stood in the hallway. "Look, you should probably go. Once Rich and Al are done here for me, the Feds are gonna swing by."

"The Feds? Like, you mean the FBI? Why?" I asked, starting down the stairs towards the lobby. While I'm sure my former boss had a decent reason, I definitely didn't want to be around to deal with law enforcement from the federal government. I could barely stomach being a private investigator.

My experience with FBI agents, limited as it was, just brought back weird sour memories of a time when I worked for Kalli and having to explain research methodology to some humorless fart my age but clearly already envisioning a trophy wife and blood pressure medication in a Florida condominium, bragging about having been an "agent" to get dates and drinks at local bars. He wanted to know how I'd managed to track down some name they'd been tracking for over two years, so obviously trying to explain my Google-fu was too much. It hadn't gone too well, I'd gotten a lecture over it somehow, and I ended up deciding the less I had to deal with federal bureaus of investigating how to flush the toilet, the better.

Kalli looked back down at her phone, texting, swiping, typing. "I might have called them once we discovered Hale was Caramello, so they're interested in what they can find."

"You 'might' have called them? Come on Kalli, really?"

"They might want the strip too, so you should get it to that Ramnee woman, out of the way. They might think it's evidence about the gold."

"Jesus, you're still on that?"

"Look, I know you don't think it's real, God fucking knows you talked about it enough to everyone who would listen when you still worked for me, but I think Caramello was a part of the gold heist, and that there's a clue as to what happened to it somewhere in his things. This apartment's the first real untouched clue in who knows how long, I gotta try it." She sighed. "Just get outta here, I'll call you tomorrow."

I walked slowly down the stairs, awkwardly holding the strip, until I got outside. In the colder air, I stood around, not knowing what to quite make of what Kalli had just said and done, and feeling, quite honestly, like this was all a little anti-climactic. I shouldn't have beens surprised honestly about Kalli wanting to get back on the whole gold thing, but it felt like just another insane level that had suddenly been added to this whole case, right at the end.

Something was bugging me as I walked off in the cool night, calling Ramnee and, after telling her the good news, listening to her rattle off instructions of where she could meet me in an hour to pick up the strip. Something that I couldn't shake off, that made me think about the other apartment, the one in the Hale name, with all that other art and all that other stuff, clearly the life that Caramello had been living by then.

Why was it hidden here?

11.

═══════════

THE KNOCKING ON THE door was consistent, but muted, someone just rapping over and over and over and over.

I groaned, rolling off the couch, spilling the cat off me. I'd gotten in finally after meeting with Helen Ramnee at some restaurant at a godforsaken hour, handing off the strip art for her to slide it, reverently, into an art case

Kalli was standing there, with an envelope and a Starbucks tray with two cups in one hand, the other now again on her ever-present phone. She shoved the tray at me, "your payment's in the envelope, I'll call you later. Gotta go, bye!" and walked off, down the hallway to the elevator. I was barely awake as I took a step back into the apartment, a tad confused, and pushed the door closed with my shoulder.

I put the coffee cups down on the desk by the computer, picking one up. I put it to my lips, and nothing came out, only a heavy THUD rattling around in the cup.

Huh, weird. I popped the cap off the cup of coffee, and a cellphone was inside.

I opened up the envelope, sliding the contents out, a check for the Manta Books job...and a piece of notebook paper, stapled to a business card. The business card was from Kalli's office, with a phone number scrawled on the back of it. The notebook paper had five words written quickly in some sort of old black marker across it, underlined.

APARTMENT BUGGED USE CUP PHONE

I went back to the phone on the desk, which was flashing. No vibrate, no ringer, just a notification blinking on the cheap smartphone's screen. I tapped the screen, still covered by the manufacturer's plastic cover, and the message came up. It was, I assumed, from Kalli.

"the fbi has your apartment bugged for some reason, use this phone to text me, its a long story ill talk to you soon if anyone asks tell them to talk call your lawyer, my lawyer, thats his number on the card"

I stared at what was, for lack of a better term, a burner phone, when a ding went off on the other side of my apartment. It was my other cellphone, as as I looked at that one in my hands, I held the other. Rob wanted to meet. He'd found something out about the strip.

What the overflowing fuck was happening in my apartment might have to wait. Hopefully, the coffee in the second cup was real, and still hot.

12.

I SAT ON THE COUCH in the back lounge of Kalli's office, the employee area where I knew she and other people who worked here sometimes slept. I figured it was as safe a place as ever, especially since apparently, my apartment was now some kind of den of spies. I'd paced around silent for a day and a half, waiting only for my payment from Manta to go through before getting cash, a bag, and taking off out the back service entrances of the building to take what I felt was a pretty complex route to throw off anyone following me.

She walked in, plopping the bag of takeout on the one table by the door.

"Seriously, you should've just stayed there, now they'll definitely know you're onto them since you're in the wind."

I picked through the bag at the lo mein and soda, "Who says that, anyway? 'In the wind'?"

"Ben I'm serious."

I cracked open one of the containers, and started digging in. "Look, come on, what're those feds going to do, they don't have any jurisdiction, it's just them probably being paranoid and wanting to steal glory about the Caramello thing." The food was from The Best Chinese, an awfully named local place, and probably one of the only Chinese food places left in Astoria.

"It may not be the FBI bugging your place." Kalli sat down at the other end of the couch, picking at her kung pow chicken and rice. "I found it when I did a random sweep of my car when I was at your place, just a quick search for listening frequencies..."

"Wait wait wait. You do what?"

"Standard stuff, now stop talking." Kalli put a hand up and continued. "Anyway, I picked up a frequency for listening, and the one I found, which was the one listening in on you," here she pointed at me, "listening in on you talking to yourself and the cat, I might add, was pretty weak and spotty. Combined with the fact that there weren't any other cars around on the block, made me realize it was from one of those spy store kits."

"Huh," I picked at some chicken and noodle, "So who, the mob? Those guys who jumped us at Hale building?"

"Jumped you," she corrected me, putting her food down. "Probably, maybe someone who's in whatever rinky-dink 'family' these guys think they are who'se always kept an ear out for the money all these years, because I'm sure some of them totally believe in it, after all these years, a sort of mafia urban legend. Hey, did you ever talk to Wagner about whatever it was he wanted to talk to you about? He's been calling here looking for you." Kalli asked me.

"Phone tag, with them getting the comic and him getting new deadlines, no time. Figured at this point it's moot, no rush, honestly."

"Yeah, I doubt that." Kalli picked up her chicken and headed out the door. "Stay here as long as you want, Ben, but figure it out." She left, leaving me sitting on the couch, by myself this time.

Part of me wanted to go back to my apartment, go through every nook and cranny in the place, find the bug or bugs, and just be a jerk screaming into them to blow out eardrums or something. Another part told me to hide out here, wait it out until Kalli or someone told me the FBI were done with the case or the mob were all swept up in a hair grease smuggling ring. A final part of me was insistent on calling Mike back to find out what he wanted, mostly to satisfy a weird itch I was feeling about this case. And as much as I hated it, that last part was going to probably win, if only to satisfy what felt like an incomplete ending.

Kalli had moved on, working with the FBI to sift through what they could about Caramello's life and tying it to anything mob-related, but I had a different dirty footpath through the comic shop I wanted to follow.

I pulled my phone out, and as I continued to shovel food in my mouth in the tiny back lounge, I texted Wagner. Time to find out what he knew and where it lay in this whole thing, I thought.

13.

"WHY CAN'T WE JUST LOOK at the copy in the book?" I was holding the Hawkblade collection that Wagner had brought with us to look at as we sat in the coffee shop. After we'd talked on the phone, I'd taken off from Kalli's office to take a roundabout route to meet up with Rob, reasonably sure I hadn't been followed. Not that I was worried about some kind of mobster, who I was reasonably sure were the group behind bugging my apartment, tailing me. I was more concerned with whatever babysitter Kalli would have tagging along, he or she would just get in the way.

"Won't show up in the book version, we need to get in close to find it. Back in the day, strips in papers were way bigger, so it'd have been easier to see." Rob and I had finally touched base about what he'd wanted to tell me, and honestly, it sounded pretty stupid.

"So what, the code is hidden in the art, and you're supposed to just figure it out? I'm not like, a crypto guy or anything, but don't you need like a master key or something to be able to work on a code?"

"But that's just it, there was a key, in the very first few strips!" Rob's theory, which some fan who knew a guy who's dad had known a guy, was that the newspaper strips had some sorta fan-aimed code hidden in them, for people to look for, secret art clues.

"What's it gonna show us then?" The waitress brought us our coffee and donuts, "Caramello's gold?"

14.

WE MET UP AT THE PUBLISHER'S office, where the last page had been taken after it went through the printer's, now up on the wall. After a lot of cajoling, Ramnee agreed to let us see it, though she wasn't happy to see us, holding a magnifying glass and wearing white cloth gloves like a museum curator. "This is ridiculous" she muttered while Wagner over the piece of paper with a magnifying glass and the flashlight from his cellphone, staring at every inch. He'd look at something on his phone once in a while, then go to look at the little notepad he'd pulled from his pocket, while I sat at someone's desk and answered irate text messages from Kalli. He talked as he worked.

"So, a guy who'd been one of the first to actively buy Hale art told a friend of mine at a con about it..."

"A what?"

"A convention, a comic book convention, wear costumes, buy books and original art, anyway! So the dude who'd been buying that original art at first..."

"Terrence Park" Ramnee chimed in. "Right, Park," Wagner continued, "So he told my friend Aisha, who's a rep for an art dealer, that he thought maybe they were watermarks and that they might be fakes he'd bought, but then like a week later, Aisha tells me that the guys calls her again, and that it's actually a code, and he'd found references to it in some early fanzines and newspapers that used to run the strip back in the day." This whole thing was starting to loop back to ridiculous, just like when it'd started, after we'd petered out and gotten a little more serious with the gangsters. I was about to close my eyes and act like I was asleep just to annoy them when Wagner spoke. "There."

I got up to walk over to the desk. He was stabbing at the paper, at one of the squiggles on the second panel, the second box. Helen Ramnee was just staring at the paper. "Holy shit." There, in the black ink swirls of someone's cape, was a small sequence of numbers, followed by a letter. Wagner was writing it down excitedly, "I told you so, I told you so! Holy shit this is so awesome! He really did it, we found the code!"

"Holy shit that's small." I could barely see it even with his finger and the light there. "How was anyone going to notice that?"

"I told you, they used to be bigger." Rob said. "You'd be surprised how big the comics section used to be in newspapers, and 'Hawkblade' was a big comic, took up almost a quarter of the page sometimes, a kid with enough time and an observant eye could definitely find this."

I snatched the paper away from him while he and the Ramnee woman talked excitedly, tuning them out. Something about going back to confirm it on all the other strips they had. I stared at the code, something simple, but easy for people to figure out. Couldn't be a book cipher, couldn't be something that would involve a lot of words.

9/6/24/2/22/G

I scrambled around on the desk for paper and a pen, writing out the alphabet and then numbering it, one through twenty-six, A through Z. I tried it.

I F X B V G

"That doesn't make any sense, it wouldn't be purposely just the alphabet" Wagner said. "That's right," Ramnee pointed to the G at the end, "That's probably the cipher, like the letter G is important. Redo it, use G as number one."

"Yeah, hold on," Rob dug through his little notebook, "My guy, he said it was usually simple and easy stuff that he'd reference in the strip before this. The last arc before this strip had to do with a missing code key involving some kind of magic letter, so, makes sense?"

I redid the numbers and letters, and this time got something else.

O L D H B

"Old HB?" Rob scratched his head. "Maybe a place he used to go to?"

"You'd know more than anyone if there was any place with those initials, if you don't recognize it..." Ramnee sighed and sat down on the desk. "That might not be the cipher, I mean, it makes sense that it is, but Old HB?"

"What's old that he had, that starts with those initials? A house, maybe?" I was spinning my wheels at this point, not entirely sure just how serious to keep taking this. For all I know, and looking at the Ramnee woman she was starting to think it too, this was just a dumb joke an old mobster has played on us all.

"Well, he did talk about his old family house in the one interview he did, but..."

"But what?" I said, perking up.

"I mean how much of that stuff is true? I mean since it turned out he was, you know, a gangster and all." Rob looked almost sheepish, like he's recommended we go try to kiss the mob guys who'd jumped me.

"Where is it?" I asked, feeling like I was going to regret this immensely.

15.

FLUSHING, DEEP IN QUEENS, was quiet, asleep. The mailbox of the house was empty, the motion sensor of the front light clicking on as we walked back and forth on the porch of the house. "Are you sure this is it?" Helen Ramnee said, peering through the window. "It doesn't look like an old house, it looks like someone lives here." It did, I thought, feeling up around the doorframe while Rob looked up and down the dark quiet street. The windows were covered but clean, the porch was clean, the door looked cheap-ish but new. There were stickers on the storm door I was holding open I realized, an American flag and a POW "We Support The Troops" one. The lawn, small as it was, was neat, cut. I felt something cool and small by the top right corner, like it was stuck down with tape, and I pulled it down. "Thought so," I smirked, holding the key up.

I clicked the door open, stepping inside quietly, the other two behind me. No alarm, no panel blinking with a silent one either, just a quiet house, mostly empty, boxes and what looked like generic rental-place footage oddly scattered around the front room. A small kitchen table, a couch, a couple of folding chairs. Ramnee walked up the stairs to the second floor while Rob and I walked into the back, towards what we realized was a kitchen, mostly empty, just a sink and the spaces for the fridge and oven.

We went back into the front living room, Rob kneeling down at the boxes. "Hawkblade books, some sketchbooks, sketchpads, photos," he handed me one, old and greyed with age in a dirty frame. It was two men in suits, posing with chests out like they were puffing up, proud and powerful. They were gangsters, I realized, one of them was probably a young Bobby Caramello. I heard Helen come back downstairs. "Nothing up there but dust and a bed you still need to put together," she said, looking around. "I don't think anyone actually lives here, it's like…"

"It's like someone moved in and then just sorta checks in once in a while" I said.

"Yeah, exactly."

"So what's here, just a bunch of his old junk? Someone else's old junk? Rob?" I turned around to look at him crouched by the boxes.

"I…" he stood up. "I don't know? I mean some of these look like they could be his old sketchbooks, and I know that some of these photos are him probably, but," he shrugged his shoulders, lowering himself back down again to sit down on the floor.

"I just wanted there to be something, you know? I mean, like in 'Hawkblade,' an adventure? God that sounds so fucking stupid, but back when I was doing all the fanzines, it was like, trying to get myself in that world, in those adventures…fuck, nevermind. It's stupid." He let himself fall to lay back on the floor with a thud, and I cocked my head. He heard it too, getting up. "I don't think this house has a basement."

We moved the boxes all against the fall wall, crouching around the spot where Wagner's head had hit the floor. The wood panels felt like they had give there, like a sponge, compared to the rest of the floor. I fumbled in my pocket for my multi-tool, sticking the knife blade into the space between two of the panels. It didn't give, but did stick up in there and Ramnee reached around to grab one of the bigger books from a box, hammering down on it, driving it into the wedge. After a few whacks, I kicked at it, and a chunk of the panels popped up. Rob pulled it and off, a single piece that had been set in like a hatch. He turned his cellphone flashlight into the gap, and we looked inside the hole.

It was a nice little cubby size, and I reached in and found the lockbox, just a little metal fireproof case, one of those that you'd keep important papers in. I shook it, the latch popping easily. Something was inside, and with Rob and Helen's phone shining on it, I opened it up, dumping papers out on the floor. She sorted through them, frowning. "They're receipts, I think." She handed one to me, the logo at the top old, some hospital in New Jersey that I didn't recognize. I picked up another one, some foundation, scanning it before I realized what they were. "They're donation receipts," I said quietly, looking up. "Look at the amounts, look how many of them."

"Holy shit," Rob said, "This is is. This was the gold, whatever he got from the bank job, he just...he just gave it all away over the years."

"What?" Helen said, "That...that doesn't make any sense."

"Probably liquidated it as soon as they could, and he took off with the whole thing instead of wanting to split it with the other guys," I said. "They never found any of the guys from that job, I'm gonna bet they're dead. I did some quick mental math, "Yeah, this looks like it's all of it, give or take a few thou, probably for one of those apartments, stuff for the fake name and background."

"So what do we do?" Rob said, "just put it all back?"

"Not much else we can do," Helen said, sweeping up the papers and putting them back in the box, putting it back in the space. "I mean, the cover's probably busted," she said, putting the chunk of floor panels back over it. Using the tool to bust it open had made a nasty crack in one of the panels, and I pushed some of the boxes over it.

We left, and I locked the front door and put the key back where I'd found it, heading back to Rob's car up the block. None of us spoke.

16.

I GOT THE PACKAGE IN the mail, with the old "my address as the sender's address, some nonsense address the sendee" trick. The Post Office and the Feds hated it, but as long as the post office still sent and delivered mail it'd still probably work.

I'd been home for a few days, not really leaving the apartment except to step into the hallway and pay the delivery guy. Kalli had messaged me to let me know the Feds had stopped caring where I was or who I was talking to, which meant they'd dropped any interest in the whole Hale/Caramello thing. It was stamped from some post office in the city, I didn't pay too much attention as I ripped the envelope open, curious.

It was a stack of comic pages with "Hawkblade By Kirby Hale" in the familiar script at the bottom left of each sheet. They were original comics, I realized, unseen ones. One smaller piece of paper fell from the bottom of the pile, and I picked it up. It was a single page from a sketchbook, thicker paper, the kind I'd seen Rob use, the script crisp and uniform capital letters, like from a comic book.

"GOT YOUR ADDRESS FROM THE INTERNET, LONG STORY. THANKS FOR NOT TOTALLY COVERING UP THE HOLE IN THE FLOOR SO I COULD GO IN AFTER YOU GUYS LEFT, I'D BEEN LOOKING FOR IT SINCE I GOT THE HOUSE. SHOULD HAVE LOOKED A LITTLE HARDER IN THERE, WOULD'VE FOUND THESE. I KEPT ONE FOR MYSELF, MEMORIES I GUESS. MY MOM TOLD ME HE'D BEEN MY DAD, I KNEW HIM AS ONE OF HER OLD BOYFRIENDS. ANYWAY, I ALWAYS LOVED COMICS. TELL ROB WAGNER I'M A BIG FAN, CAN'T WAIT TO SEE HIS HAWKBLADE WORK. – RICK MELLO"

Well.

That explained who was maintaining the house.

Late Arrivals

"Drums"

I WAS IN FLUSHING, walking towards the deli, taking a route around the other block, the one on the far side of my house, not really in any sort of hurry to go get a sandwich and a drink. There was no food in the house, which, as a grown man in his thirties house-sitting, should have been a sign that this month wasn't going to be going my way. I normally didn't like venturing too far back into Queens these days, the bus service you needed to rely on getting shittier and shittier, it seemed, but Adam and Mal had asked nicely, and I'd known Adam on and off forever. He was one of the few guys outside of work I was friends with, even if I we really only saw each other once or twice a year at backyard cookouts or weddings. Mal I didn't know, but he seemed nice enough, so whatever, house sit, watch the cat they claimed needed a special diet, enjoy their central air during a hot summer.

There was just the issue of food. Apart from cat food, that is.

I saw it on the other side of the street as I walk walking back, actually, set in the metal-barred, white-painted fence of one of the houses in the middle of the block. I'd gotten a six-pack of root beers, a few sandwiches, and a large bag of no-name chips. That should hold me for a few days I'd thought, when I saw it. A photo in a frame, old and tarnished but taken care of, with dried old flowers stacked around the sidewalk. I crossed over, because hey, why not. The house was just like every other house on the block with the partial metal fence around the front yard, less a barrier and more of a clear line to keep dogs from shitting on lawns. Driveway too, house nice, red brick, two stories, cared for, but obviously not new. The window frames looked at least a dozen years old, the driveway patched. It was, I realized, a legacy, the kind of house that had the same family living in it for years, probably since the seventies when this area was a solid middle-class area full of mostly Irish union members or firefighters, some Greek painters and construction workers, and a smattering of Chinese and Dominican families. Whoever lived here had been here for a while, enough to see Flushing turn over more than a few times.

I looked back at the picture, at the flowers. Whoever she was, smiling and blonde and green-eyed in some kind of dress, maybe, it was hard to tell in the faded image, she'd been young when the picture was taken, maybe forty years ago? It looked like the kind of glamor pictures people took back then at Sears, a group shop and some portraits of each family member to scatter around, you in your holiday or Sunday best, posed smiling, cheerful, full of promise, a reminder of some kind of potential. Underneath the picture written in the frame, engraved, was "Forever In Our Hearts". The picture frame was attached to the metal bars with wrapped wire punched through the frame, dirty and rusted with time, probably something from someone's garage. The rust had turned the loops into solid little chunks of solder, it'd been there so long, which explained the tarnish of the metal frame and the fade of the photo.

I heard the creak of metal, the front door opening, and I hustled off, not wanting to look like I was snooping. I turned a corner as soon as I could, not wanting to get caught snooping. A few minutes later I was back at Adam and Mal's house, planting bags on the kitchen table and pouring out a scoop of cat food for Busty, who meowed at me from her perch on the kitchen counter. She head-butted me when I got closer, and I scratched her behind the ears for a bit before she tried to nip at my hand, leaping down to the floor with a thud. "Fat little fuck," I murmured to no one, going back to my sandwiches. I scrolled through my phone and clicked on some video a friend sent me of some guy trying to light fireworks and setting his hair on fire, and I laughed, chewing on half of an Italian sub, the vinegar seeping out onto my other hand.

Who was that girl in the picture? You didn't see much of that in this kind of neighborhood, the shrines to lost family members. There'd briefly been one further up towards one of the bigger boulevards I knew a few years ago, candles and flowers by the curb where some guy had been run over by a hit-and-run crossing the street. Did she die in 9/11? You occasionally saw those around, but no, I thought, cleaning up and laying on the couch in the living room, flicking on the TV for nothing in particular, those are different. It usually tells you they died then, because it's important to make it stand out, festooned usually with American flags, I thought, scratching my chin.

My phone dinged, and I looked down at the message.

AT WORK AT THE BAR COME BY

I sighed, thinking about it for a minute before I rolled off the couch, clicking off lights and making sure the cat hadn't gotten up the stairs, something Adam and Mal had been insistent on, and heading out, stuffing my keys, phone, and wallet into my pockets. Alex was another old friend, someone from high school I'd run into recently and started talking to again. She'd invited me by the bar she worked a few times, so fuck it, why not, I thought. I started walking up to the main boulevard, looking back down the one block I'd come up from earlier, where the house with the picture in the fence was, thinking about that girl as the bus pulled up and I got on.

"So how're Adam and Mal?" Alex asked me as I walked in a little while later, leaning over from behind the bar. "I haven't seen them in forever." We'd all briefly been a single group of friends when I first started college, that odd attempt people do when they try to combine their different groups of friends, to mixed results. I played with a coaster, distracted. "OK, I guess, if they're doing a month off."

The bar was quiet, a Wednesday night, allowing us a little bit of privacy. We'd chatted about life since the last time we'd seen each other. I was a couple of years into working for myself as a private eye, which she found hilarious, she had a kid she adored, and I'd helped my parents pack up the old house and move to Philadelphia to be closer to some family that lived there from my mom's side. We were over a decade past high school but not much had changed otherwise, to be completely honest. Still dumb, still hanging out in Queens and thinking about how much it sucked to have to take the N or the 7 train, how the buses never worked, and rent looking like it was going to go up again, probably because of fucking Manhattanites. Alex lived with her kid and her dad in the house she grew up in, he'd had been a fireman and had driven us as kids to parties and concerts, mostly just happy his daughter had friends and that she didn't hate him, I guess. She still sometimes sang in local bands, and she bartended and co-managed Sunshine Bar & Grill, the place that used to be Deliah's, the bar we'd always gone to that didn't ask too many questions about ID when we were teenagers and bored on Saturday nights, drinking overpriced beers and shots of vodka, thinking we were hard.

"Hey, so I was walking back from the deli, you know the one by the park near where I am? They have the sandwiches?"

"The Corona Street, yeah," she said, drinking from a bottle of water, "that's by Linda's house, you remember, Linda Pullman? She was in that cult, had a crush on you? She got married, moved in with Bashir, had some kids." I did, the cute hippie girl who ended up in some weird Christian revival movement she tried to get various people from school to go to with her. I'd heard she'd OD'ed and left Queens, running across her name randomly during some work a few years back, so good to hear that was wrong. Bash had been the guy we all bought weed and bootleg movies from back then, a weird pairing, but whatever. I pushed the coaster across the bar, "So I'm walking and I see this picture attached to someone's fence, like, a memorial? It's got flowers everywhere, it's like a block up from the Corona? You know what it is?"

"It's that girl got killed back in like, the seventies," a voice answered from next to me, an older man nursing a beer, "the Kimball place, right, red brick? That's where Janet Kimball's family still lives, girl died back in like, shit," he looked down, counting on his hand, "I think seventy-three?"

Made sense, I thought, picture looked like it was thirty, almost forty years old in a frame like that, made sense for the house, a family home around since the sixties or seventies in that one spot while Queens slowly changed around them. The conversation started to change, and Alex and I made vague but close-enough plans for me to come by next time she was working and get a late dinner when her shift finished. I walked back towards the house in the dark, no real speed or purpose through the neighborhood, letting my feet and the fact that I was somehow, still sober, taking me where they should. I ended up back at that fence, back at that picture in the metal bars, looking a little better, a little less dirty and forgotten in the dark. There was a light on in the house on the second floor, a flicker blue-white light from a TV. Someone couldn't sleep. Someone probably didn't sleep much anymore, probably not since the seventies, especially now realizing that life was getting closer and closer to ending and nothing was going to bring her back.

Shit, maybe I was drunk.

"She was dating Walter Fredericks, his dad owned the one paper mill by where all the subways park now, but back then it was like, mostly just factories. The subway hadn't expanded that far yet to the water." My dad's sister Fiona said, stubbing out her cigarette as we sat on her screened-in porch. I knew where she was talking about, a weird pseudo-industrial area right before the subways dipped underground to go under the river into Manhattan, an area slowly transforming now into an amalgamation of restaurants, condos, and small businesses, all under the shadow of the ConEd and bank high-rises built there forever, clear delineations that you're at the edge of Queens.

She paused to take a sip of coffee and look at her cellphone, checking the time. "Hot date?" I joked, finishing my coffee. Fiona smiled, "actually, yes, Lucille is coming by to pick me up so we can go visit Donald and his new wife. Anyway," she continued, "Walter Fredericks ended up owning that factory, his family was very wealthy, back then? That factory employed a lot of people, and everyone knew that he was going to run it, which he did. In the eighties he turned it into a plastic factory, they made plastic flowers, cups, plates there."

"Huh."

"Anyway, it was in the news, she disappeared one night, big scandal, her parents were on the radio and even the TV about it. Terrible stuff. Walter eventually retired and sold the factory, sold his house, moved to Florida like five years ago." My gut started to sink as she kept talking and lit another cigarette, "The new owners looked in the basement and found a big drum, like a metal one you'd use for like, sewage from the plant?" Fiona looked at me, leaning forward. "The poor girl was inside, he'd killed her and left her in the basement of his house the whole time because she wouldn't get an abortion. Terrible, you know? Anyway, they, the police I guess, went down to Florida to interview Walter, but he'd heard what happened, so when they got there he was dead." She put a finger like a gun to her temple, "He'd killed himself. He was old, I'm sure that he did not want to spent the remainder of his years in jail." A car pulled up to the curb, honking, and my aunt got up, stubbing her smoke out. "I'll see you soon? That's Lucille."

"Yeah, for sure," I said, getting up to hug her goodbye, my dad's weird hippie sister. She left in the car with her friend as I stood on her steps, walking slowly back to the bus to get back to Adam and Mal's place. The bus left me far enough away that I passed by the Kimball house again on my way back, and I stopped to look at the picture. "I'm sorry," I said, half-aloud, snapping up in surprise when someone coughed, seeing an older woman unloading groceries from the back of her car, staring at me. Shit.

"I'm sorry," I said again, louder, walking away, face red as I turned the corner unnecessarily to get out of there and back towards Adam and Mal's, finally getting there to sit on their front stoop before going in. I thought about the girl in the drum, about the plastic factory by the river, about the old man in Florida finding out from someone's nephew who told his mom who told her aunt who called him that they'd found something in the basement of his old house, and him immediately thinking of a .22 he kept in the kitchen for home defense, about the cops coming for an old man who'd fucked up real back almost forty years back.

I thought about what house he grew up in, which house was the Fredericks house from back then.

I thought about whether or not Adam and Mal had a large basement, and if somewhere in there in a half-forgotten dusty corner I could find the top of a metal drum tossed aside in a curious moment, trying to see what would have been in the metal container hidden under the basement stairs for all that time.

"Hot Hard Heat"

1

The wet oppressive heat of the summer weighed down like so much water despite the unbearable sun, and Ben felt his shirt soaking through his back and the center of his chest immediately as he walked out of the office and down the block to the subway. "Fuck," he muttered, one more thing to have to deal with. Things had been bad enough that he'd gone back to work for Kalli Kiliaris at her detective agency, which wasn't too bad considering how much unofficial work he'd done for her before, but the indignity of having to make it formal and long-term annoying him slightly. But a slight annoyance on a day like today was enough to make him even madder, so he hustled and stood among everyone else on the subway platform, staring at his phone, looking at the information he'd been sent.

The majority of the cases she dealt with were divorce stuff, extra manpower for boring federal stuff like babysitting witnesses, and occasionally tracking down missing spouses or teenagers who'd taken the fuck off for greener pastures, but enough were strange that sometimes when Ben had gone out on his own that she'd throw them his way as a favor, as well as to build a layer between her and the case should things go to shit. Her agency had a lot of weight behind its name thanks to her dad and then her work, and sometimes having a stringer wasn't such a bad idea, Ben had admitted to himself on occasion when thinking of his old boss.

This was not one of those cases, nor was it one of those times when he admired his former-now-current again boss as he rode the train into Manhattan. Kalli still maintained offices in Queens despite rising rent and the hipsters turning every corner into a bistro or a juice bar, having pulled together enough cash to just up and buy the block. The train roared into the tunnel and for a moment, Ben thought about what it meant to be able to just gather enough raw cash to straight-up buy the property...then moved on. Better to not bother, not that Kalli was dirty in any way, but she and her close circle had their ways and means, and in the end, Ben Miles was just one more piece for her to move around to get things done.

The phone screen still showed what she'd sent him despite losing signal, and he again looked at the text and small shot of a man's face, blown up as much as could be and still be identifiable. Hector Nunez was twenty-one, until recently had worked doing basic data entry at a startup in an office building in Long Island City, and like most employees of a place that closes down, took home a bunch of office supplies and equipment to supplement that last paycheck, filling up the back of a friend's car. It honestly wasn't the worst thing in the world, Ben thought, considering how much he'd lifted from various jobs, except for what he'd ended up taking in that batch of printer paper, pens, a TV, a computer or two, a printer/scanner, and a box of miscellaneous junk.

The train continued and Ben jumped across the platform at a station to change, and then ten minutes later walking through Times Square to another train, heading even further uptown, in Manhattan now, aiming for Washington Heights. "They told everyone on Monday it was the last week, that night he emailed his bosses and told them he was cashing in his sick days," Kalli had said earlier in her office. "Apparently he called someone and was the last to leave that night, emptied out a conference room or office or whatever not many people used, took the desktop units in there, figured no one would notice."

"I don't blame him," Ben had said, leaning back in his chair, "I mean, what did I take when I quit the last time I worked here?"

"A case of copy paper and all the coffee and filters," Kalli didn't bother looking up as she clicked at her computer, "There, sent you the email with what you need. The computers in there were apparently used specifically for the company's network or something, I honestly don't know, just that they hadn't been wiped so they're full of sensitive login stuff and whatever." Ben had stood up, "Why not just call the cops? I mean, only a sucker sneezes at work, but, this is sorta....ehhh?" He waved a hand flat up and down, tilting his head.

"Weird? Well," Kalli also stood up and walked over to the office door, slowly closing it before answering quietly, "The sale and closing were not popular, and there's...a few issues of legality. Nothing I can say no to, but enough that it shouldn't really be a paper trail, especially with police."

"Hell of a thing to take on."

She'd shrugged, opening the door. "Gotta keep the lights on, you know?" He'd walked through, turning back. "Is...are things OK?"

"Look, just do this one, help me out, and I swear the next few will be interesting at least, OK?" Kalli had away towards someone else, and Ben had left, into that heat, and was now in the still crisp sterile air of the subway station, waiting for a train to take him uptown. He hated it, hated shaking down guys for what was basically nonsense, something like this. The chances were more than likely that the computers, which according to the email numbered three, were already wiped and two of them sold somewhere or traded, which means he'd have to try to trick or bully his way into finding out where they went to confirm each one. "Fuck," he said, just out loud enough that the man standing next to him as the train pulled in stepped away a second, looking at Ben oddly.

2

The inside of the train car was quiet considering the time of day, and Ben sat down, thinking about the approach. He knew it wouldn't be that hard, there were enough white guys in Washington Heights that he wouldn't stand out, but he also knew that the real obstacle was physically trying to get into Hector's building. The address had him down in one of the older converted ones, which meant no doorman but a lot of foot traffic, open windows on the ground level...and a buzzer on the door that might be high-tech enough for a fob.

The sun was still high when he came aboveground, but the breeze he felt blowing up the street made it seem like a different planet from oppressive and humid Queens, and he took a second to jump into a hip store selling overpriced iced coffee, relying on cute college girls to get suckers to pay that much and tip generously...which Ben did, asking about how long the place had been there.

"We just opened like, a year ago, I've been here for six months," Asia, who was a student, said, "Are you from around here?"

"Queens but looking to move up here, know any older buildings? I figured I'd go grab the numbers off the side for the owners, you know?" He smiled, and she pointed out and down to the left. "Other side of the block over there's some, good luck!" she said as the woman behind Ben stepped up to order. He put two dollar bills in the tip cup and left, sipping his coffee, walking left...away from where he knew he had to go. Might as well enjoy the day, might as well see what the whole neighborhood was like, too. Ben meandered for a good half-hour, up and down, acting both like he knew where he was going, but not in a hurry, around every block for four blocks around the subway stop. Finally, he turned the corner, heading towards Hector's building. He stood in front of the door, staring at the screen and then the buzzer system like he was waiting for someone, buzzed a number, and waited. The older men by the curb in their folding chairs were actively yelling about something in the summer heat, and again, Ben felt stupid in pants and his button-up shirt, but at least he wasn't the older man in a full suit who opened the front door of the apartment building, smiling for Ben. "You go!" he said, motioning. Ben stepped in quickly, up the two steps into the lobby, nodding and murmuring a quick "thanks gracias" as he strode, calmly but with purpose, for the stairs.

It worked well enough in his neighborhood, he'd thought, that of course it worked here, because everyone was trusting in the summer. No one wants to be stuck waiting in the heat, if you were around and acted like you were waiting to get in because you were expected or lived there someone would inevitably chip in or open a door, the adage about New Yorkers acting mean and unfriendly only applying to tourists and assholes, he thought. He walked up to the third floor thinking about how many people he'd probably let into the building that hadn't lived there, guests, sales people, door-to-door Jehovah's Witnesses who turned away when Ben opened his apartment door and they realized he wasn't Spanish. He walked behind a man in a pale blue t-shirt who'd paused on the stairs to check a phone, and Ben stayed half a step behind, lingering to also "check" his phone before looking up to see him open up apartment 4B and Ben walked up one more flight before softly turning around, back down to 4B and Hector.

"Hector, man," Ben said, knocking on the door. "It's about work." He knocked again, and a woman walked down the stairs, smiling at Ben before continuing, the older woman's arms laden with plastic bags full of containers, and Ben thought about where she could be going as he leaned against the door. "Dude I literally just saw you go in here, come on, be cool, it's fucking boiling," he continued. "Not a cop, promise." There was a shuffle behind the door, like someone had been standing there and holding something, and the heavy muffled THUNK of the bolt being thrown was heard before Hector opened the door, peering out. "Figured someone would show up, yeah, come in." Hector was skinny with glasses and a trimmed beard, every inch the hipster programmer the picture showed, some kind of cartoon character of a mad scientist on his shirt. Ben walked in and saw the baseball bat by the doorway, and headed in. At his feet a small dog dashed around, "Prince, stop," Hector said, and the dog yapped, sitting down and staring up. "Good boy," he said, scooping up the small mutt and carrying him. "So what, they want it all back?" Hector said sitting on the large leather sci-fi looking chair in the living room that swiveled away from facing the TV, the remnants of takeout on the glass coffee table. Chicken and rice and some plantains, Ben could smell it, and it reminded him how hungry he was. "What are you, like from the new owners?"

Ben sat down on the couch, hands on his knees. "Not quite, they hired my boss, and my boss got me to do it." Hector put the dog down, "Like a detective? Shit, that's...for real?"

"Yeah, for real."

"I mean," he lifted his arms up, "Why? You know like my last check wasn't even a full one, right? A bunch of people I know told me yesterday they all got severance packages, but the data people like me, we got shit. Who cares? I'm gonna get a job at Best Buy," Hector said, frustrated and standing up, "'cause tech is mad fucking racist, fuck this shit." He sat back down, head down. "I got the stuff in the bedroom in the back, the computers."

"Look, if we're being honest," Ben said uncomfortably, feeling like he'd just somehow crushed this kid's whole day, "I just gotta make sure they're wiped, something about the logins to a bunch of servers or something?" Hector looked up, confused. "Huh? No, the server access was on the floor below me. The fun programmers and everyone was fifteenth floor, I was fourteenth with the rest of us that did the actual hard work, and below that was storage and the servers. This was just, like, a conference room with some desktops? I'd never been in it, it was usually dark. I don't know, I never went to conference meetings." Hector again stood up, this time to walk into the kitchenette of the small apartment. "Look, my mom's gonna be home soon, can we like, hurry up? I don't want her thinking I'm in trouble. I'm not in...I'm not in trouble, right?" Hector said, and Ben nodded. "I...I don't think so? Shit, OK can we like, turn them on, see what's on them?"

"Yeah, I mean, I got them all plugged in, was gonna literally wipe them later today." The two went into the back of the apartment, into the smaller of two bedrooms made even more cramped with the piles of clothes, a few cardboard boxes of various office supplies, posters on the walls, an old iPod on the bed...and three monitor desktops perched precariously on pillows, all plugged into an overworked power strip. "Here," Hector pressed buttons on the side of each one, and the three flicked to life. "I mean it shouldn't show anything, just tell us that we're not connected to the internet really," Hector said, "Maybe ask for us to log into the...huh."

"Huh?" Ben leaned forward, "What's 'huh' mean?"

"Well they're like, telling me to log in, right? But that," he pointed to the string of numbers and letters above the little box for entering text, "wasn't our network."

3

Ben walked through the door and in the dark, nothing felt better even as he heard the industrial thrum of the air conditioner going, the space too old and probably drafty to really effectively contain cold air. Still, Bobby put a cold beer on the bartop in front of him and proceeded to pour the two of them shots. "Cheers, eh?"

"Man, you have no idea," Ben knocked his back, relaxing in front of the beer as Bobby moved onto the other regulars. The Old Time was quiet, it was not that clean and not that popular with anyone who didn't live in the neighborhood, and a guy with two fingers missing from one hand hung out in front of the bar at night hustling coke and pills to the college students who dared to come in. But no one except day-drinking regulars were there at four in the afternoon on a Tuesday, which let Ben stare at his phone and the long list of notes on the pages of his little notebook that Hector has rattled off to him. It was a ton of computer mumbo-jumbo as far as he was concerned, but the gist of it, which he was still trying to wrap his head around, was starting to concern him a little.

"Hey Bobby," Ben asked as the bartender drifted past him, "You ever buy anything online? Like, click an ad and shit?"

"I don't know, probably, why?"

"You ever wonder like, if the ads online are bad or something, putting whatever, some kinda spying shit on your phone or computer?" Ben sipped his beer, staring at his own phone on the bartop. "I guess, but that shit's always spying on you, you know? 'Sides, I've dropped like, I don't know, four phones? Can't spy on me if I'm always replacin' 'em," he winked moving down towards the middle-aged wine mom nursing two glasses at the far end, leaving Ben alone again in the coolness of the room, thinking about what Hector had tried to tell him.

4

"So where's the stuff?" Kalli said on the other end of the line as Ben leaned casually against the door, up on his buiding's roof. It was still too hot to do anything really, and the little air conditioner unit he had would cool the bedroom of his apartment and that was it, so he'd been spending evenings before the sun went down up on the roof, reading or playing on his phone when he wasn't working, enjoying any bit of breeze and non-humidity that he could get compared to the swamp that his apartment felt like.

"Can I come in and talk to you about this?" He replied, letting himself slide down to sit, back against the dirty old metal of the door, sighing. "No you can't, come on Ben, where are the computers? Was the kid not there?"

"Look, something came up to make it weird, so I got a lead on them, OK?" Something was up, Ben thought, because normally Kalli was never losing her cool, and sometimes was even willing to come along for the weird cases he took, just to get out from behind the desk. This was different, and he needed some space and time on it, on that tone of hers and the way she'd looked tired when he'd last been there and why she'd be willing to take on something semi-shady so officially. "Fine," she said, "Look, you're good, despite what I tell you sometimes and what everyone else tells you all the time, and you're like my brother, but please don't fuck around, OK? Lemme know when you have something."

"OK yeah," he said, hitting END on the phone and standing up. "Fuck me, man," he said, stretching. Kalli was always on the level, always, and after talking to Hector some more earlier he'd felt like this was only getting worse. He reached into his pocket, feeling the plastic of the access card Hector had given it to him, "borrowed," from someone else, the younger man now fully-invested in figuring whatever this was out. Time to go to work, and see if he could still get into the building "to get one last thing from my desk, you know?" he said out loud, trying to get the tone sounding just right.

It worked, later that day, when he knew the security guard at the door would not care that much on a Friday afternoon right before the end of his shift and a fifty helped him get into the elevators with a promise to be right out, "I promise man, I don't want to get you in trouble, bro."

The building was a mix of abandoned hallways of not-open-yet startups, empty rooms that were property squatting by people he figured didn't even live in New York, and bustling offices where one floor was a video game company where two young men, one blond and one dark-haired wearing glasses with no lenses had stared at him briefly and awkwardly, and another seemed like some sort of lifestyle brand where handsome people either lounged around or furiously were at work at computers, nowhere near leaving. "Shit," he said softly to himself. Doesn't anyone go home on Friday? Still, Hector had told him the building had a lot of turnover, so if he was vague but sounded right enough, he'd be able to navigate the building.

"Can I help you?" someone said as Ben stood by the elevator bank twenty minutes after "wandering," turning around to find a young woman with a phone in her hand in neon-blue tights and a flannel shirt peering at him. "Are you here for a meeting with Craig?" She looked back at her phone, as if confirming something, and Ben put his hands in his pockets, "Nah, my boss manages the office on the fifth floor, keeps it clean, he sent me today, sorry. I was just being nosy," he said, figuring a dash of honesty didn't hurt. "Wanted to see who else in this building. IT's pretty cool, looks slick. What do you guys do here?" he said pointing at the space of computer banks through the glass wall behind her. She turned around, "Oh, customer service for a startup, I'm sorry, it's cool. I thought you were the new assistant office manager coming in, but," she held up her phone to him, the photo of someone much younger than Ben, black, with thick sky-blue framed glasses on his face, "Clearly, you're not him," she said. "Yeah, this is just an offsite location."

"Oh, that's cool," he hit the button, as if uninterested, "So like these companies don't always just have one spot or office?" She chuckled, "No way, most of this building is offsite stuff for these companies." She paused, "What floor did you say your boss managed, what office?" The elevator dinged and Ben got on, "Anyway, sorry for bothering you, thanks!" he said hurriedly, hitting the button for the first floor, and as the doors closed, he hit the one of the floor right below, seven, getting off and walking straight down past another glass wall towards the stairwell, and taking that four flights up. "Fuckin' need to work out," he grunted as he came out into the tenth floor, pausing. It was quiet, empty still, like Hector thought it'd be, but he could see the red lights of locked electronic doors. Ben took out Hector's card, and holding his breath, waved it at the first lock.

Pressed it against the flat metal panel about the size of the card.

Again, nothing.

"Come the fuck on," he whispered, hearing steps at the stairwell door next to him, standing up and turning to face it as the door swung open and the girl from the office stood there. "OK, so who are you?" Ben smiled and put up his hands, and in hers he could see her phone up, camera going...and in the other her keys, the long metal spike of something from a keychain sticking out between her knuckles. "Look, I'm sorry," he took a step back, "I work for a lady, she hired me to find a guy, he thought he left something I need here, he lent me his card from when he worked here, I figured I'd just pop by and get it."

She stared at him, and put her phone down after a moment, unclenching the keys from her other fist. "Whatever," she muttered, "Lin," as she pulled a card from her shirt pocket and slid it into a slot on the side of the lock. "Huh?"

"Lin, like Lindsey."

"Oh, uh...Ben," he said, awkwardly as the lock beeped softly and there was an audible click. "I fucking hate working here anyway," she said and stepped aside.

"Thanks," Ben said, stepping into the office, taking his own phone out and sliding the flashlight function on. "Wanna, I don't know, come in?" he swept the light around the empty office, realizing now he was in the dark, that none of the ones he'd seen had any windows at all. Just artificial light and sound and recirculated air for however many hours you'd be at work, he thought. "Sure whatever, I said I was going for coffee" he heard from behind him, a second light sweeping around. "So like, what are you looking for? What do you even do?"

"Find stuff, look for people, usually for myself on my own, but, you know, time's rough, I do it for someone else."

"The cops?"

"Fuck no, my boss. She's cool, works with cops sometimes, but no, not directly cops. You know who used to work here?" He looked around at the skeletal remains of emptied desks, their drawers either pulled out entirely or left open. A few cables peeked out from around corners or on top of desk space where computers and power strips had sat, but he realized most of the large singular room was empty.

"Yeah, heard they got bought out, figured honestly there'd be someone on this floor no matter what, but after a while they just left. You used to hear a lot of traffic from this floor, I think they had people like, twenty-four seven?"

"Aren't you like four floors down or whatever? How'd you hear anyone?" Ben knelt by one desk, the one with the chipped corner that Hector had told him to look for. Feeling underneath it, he found the key, taped to the underside, the key to the conference room. "You know, tech culture, I'm fucking running for coffee and doing grunt work for crunch while they all do Insta live broadcasts and shit when they should be answering emails." Shining the light around, he saw the conference rooms against the far wall, "So just, being around. You knew anyone named Hector who worked here?"

At the name he could feel her brighten up, "Yeah, he's cool. Cute, too. You working for him?" Ben tried the key in the first door, feeling resistance. "Not exactly, more like, I was looking for him and that led me here." The second door opened, and Ben stepped aside. "I'll buy you a drink and tell you all about it, sound cool?"

She made a face, "Sure, whatever," and stepped into the conference room.

5

"I hate it," Lin said as she and Ben sat in the diner, the Friday night crowd streaming by. They'd gone a few blocks further than he'd wanted to into a gentrified stretch that was mostly overpriced brownstones, but she'd wanted to get away from anywhere her coworkers might see them, finding the faux-retro place that was definitely a chain trying hard not to be a chain tucked between a pet grooming place and an Iranian joint that was staffed by nothing but what looked like white college dropouts. "I studied digital literacy and like, this is all I could find for months that wasn't serving." Lin was almost thirty and told Ben that this was her last stab at something tech-related before saying fuck it and moving back home and getting a municipal job, as they both stabbed at plates of burgers and fries and he sucked down a ginger ale and she nursed a float that had too many ingredients listed on the menu. "I mean, you could always get a PI job," he joked, after she'd gotten the full story from him. "I thought you were like, a reporter for one of those blogs snooping around or whatever, honestly," she said, "It's why I followed you. Figured catching it might help me get noticed."

"Like a blogger?"

"Look, most tech outlets worth a damn are all online, don't you know anything?" Lin smirked, "Hey, I gotta go home, but seriously, if you need like, help, is there a job or something in this for me?"

She stood up and scooped up her phone off the too-clean table surface, crossing her arms. Ben scratched his chin, "I mean, I could put in a good word for you, you know? I don't know if she's looking to hire, but like, never hurts."

"Honestly, anything would be better than this place, doing customer service for fucking grocery deliveries," she said, striding out of the diner and immediately on her phone, "Call me!"

Ben watched her leave, and then thought about the messenger bag next to him he'd bought in a hurry from a small store that sold luggage, t-shirts, and posters of superheroes from comic books and firefighters standing in front of American flags, needing something to carry it around.

In the dark of the former office he'd found stacks of boxes full of t-shirts, the cheap kind printed en mass as giveaways, bearing the company logo...as well as another box of t-shirts with a logo and name he'd seen elsewhere. Elsewhere in this building. "Hey, this is downstairs, right?" he'd said, motioning for Lin to look at. "Yeah but they fuckin' suck, I used to play their games. This is the new version after the original company went bankrupt, someone else bought them and bought the name and logo basically. Some investment firm or other company."

"So that's common?"

"Oh yeah, we've had two ownership changes in the two years I've been at my job and there'd been like three before that," she had said, "I'm sure there's like twenty or thirty studios or offices in here and like four companies own all of it. Maybe even the building too," she said, and then had pointed. "What's that?"

6

He'd grabbed it and they'd left, and now as Ben got up as well from the diner and paid, making sure the new bag was slung cross-body to keep it from being snatched off him, he thought about what Hector had told him, about their Internet network and about how some of the computers connected to something else. He took his phone out, texting something, walking out and almost bumping into two young men standing at the entrance to the diner. "Sorry," he said, "No it's OK man, don't worry about it," one said, tall and blond and dressed fashionably, but in a way that Ben realized was made to look like he was poor and half-thrown together.

Ben's phone beeped and Hector had responded. Yes, it was possible what he'd asked, and more than likely, now that he thought about it, especially since he'd tried to access whatever it was through the computers he'd taken but it didn't work, like they were just backups or older versions, not that it mattered because someone's cousin had them and was wiping them to use for gaming or whatever.

Then the phone rang, Ben answering it, Hector on the other end of the line. "So I'm gonna get outta here, some white guy's been lurking around here, watching my building? And not like, you, you're cool, and he doesn't live here, he just, hangs out?" Ben sighed, "Look, just be cool, it's fine. It's fucking computer stuff and nerds," he said, before Hector cut him off, "No no, man, you don't get it, it's a lot of money riding on these sales and stuff? I've been like, doing research? My company got bought out by the building owners, which is weird, because like, weren't we paying rent to them or something? Isn't that like a conflict of interest?"

"A what? And what the hell do you mean 'lurking,' he's probably just a drug dealer, you know how white guys are. Look, I'm serious, Hector, relax. Ditch those computers, get a new job, be cool, relax, it's fine. Everything's fine," he said, turning to step into the subway station and again bumping into someone. "What the f…"

"Sorry sorry!" a voice said, and it was the two from the diner, "We just, uhhh…" the one said, "Sorry, I saw your bag, it's real retro, where'd you get it?" he gushed, the other nodding.

"What?" Ben stared, confused, "Fuck man I don't know, over there," he said, pointing at the small storefront across the street, turning around and stepping down the stairs to the train. "I gotta go, I'll be in touch soon, OK? Stay still, don't go any…hello? Fuck!" Ben realized Hector had hung up. He thought about texting Kalli, then thought better of it. He walked back up the stairwell, looking around, and seeing the drug store with WE SELL STAMPS and ATM INSIDE 99 CENT FEE signs in the window, jogged across the street towards it, thinking about where he could find a postbox.

He had to ask Kalli something.

7

Normally, Ben later thought, he'd have been in the bedroom the night they threw the firebomb through the window, but this night he'd fallen asleep at the desk in the living room watching TV and trying to text Hector, who wasn't responding. Shit.

It'd been two things actually, the first not a brick but a piece of concrete, smashing the second-story apartment window facing the street and skittering across the floor as he awoke and fell back out of the chair and hit the floor, rolling over. Two seconds after that, he felt it, the heat of something small and heavy and on fire right there, rolling around, the sound of a glass bottle on the floor. It hadn't broken.

"Fuck!" Ben jumped up, running across the apartment to the kitchenette as the flaming bottle rolled around on the uneven ancient apartment floor, digging under the sink for the fire extinguisher. Hurriedly he pulled the pin, spraying it down as gas sloshed around in it, the rag stuck in the neck of the dark-green whiskey bottle burned to almost nothing. He looked out the window, a risky move, but saw enough to see two people running down the dark quiet Queens street. "What the fuck!" he barked, dropping the extinguisher and snatching up his keys and the small metal cylinder in the dish by the door, went out the apartment, down the stairs taking them two at a time, turning, dashing off after them, seeing two figures down the block headed towards the bigger boulevard. "Those guys tried to blow my fucking house up!" he yelled at no one in particular as he passed a crowd outside the Irish bar, smoking cigarettes. "Fuckin' grab them!" he said half-out of breath at a couple who were staring at the two running, and then Ben dashing full-tilt pell-mell down the block.

They'd slowed down, not realizing he was after them, thinking he was either calling 911 or still putting out the fire. The metal cylinder, snug in one fist, super-illegal, he thought, flicked out to a foot and change in length, secured from a guy's trunk in a diner in New Jersey, black non-reflective metal. Not a true asp baton, but close enough, and he raised it up as the first guy on that corner turned around where they stood catching their breath, and came down hard on the blond one's shoulder.

"SHIT!" he screamed and fell, the black-haired one was already trying to run while Ben cocked a foot back and kicked the blond one in the side under the ribs, "Fucking assholes! What the fuck!" He turned to see the other again halfway down the block, and took off after him, in a rage now, cocking his arm back and throwing the collapsible baton wildly, sending it spinning forward to hit the black-haired guy in the back, making him pause enough to turn and see Ben barreling into him, head down, full-speed.

A car screeched as the two rolled into the street and Ben felt something wet on his forehead and left arm, probably the rough concrete scraping him, but he'd locked his arms around the black-haired guy and didn't let go, pulling and squeezing and trying to punch the screaming guy wherever he could, adrenaline surging through him. Behind him he heard someone yelling, "Stop fuck sorry! We're sorry man let him go!" and it was the blond-haired one, his one arm held wrong, the shoulder either dislocated or broken. A crowd had gathered, assuming it was another drunk fight, slowly moving on as Ben slowed, letting go of the black-haired guy and pushing him away as he stood up. He cocked a fist back and approached the blond one, standing there in fashionable tight pre-ripped jeans, white, a floppy t-shirt just the right kind of oversized covered in a print that looked like paint stain over and over under a denim jacket. The black-haired one stood up as well, dressed sort of the same, the kind of casual sloppiness that Ben associated with money and art school, and the two stood there, unsure about what to do now.

"Man, just, give us the thing, alright? I'm sorry, nothing happened, it's cool, we'll call my dad…"

"What the FUCK is wrong with you!" Ben yelled and took an aggressive step forward, wishing he had the baton on him, realizing it was in the gutter a block or so back. "You tried to firebomb my fucking place!" They looked appropriately shamed, Ben realized, like two kids caught joy-riding on a lawnmower, and he realized why they looked familiar. "You're from that fucking office, aren't you, the, the…" he snapped his fingers, hands shaking, coming down.

"Unreality Games," the dark-haired one said.

"What are you, fucking enforcers?" Ben said sarcastically, and felt like a goon, realizing that these two were Lin's age and probably also interns and he'd cracked one's shoulder and probably bruised the ribs of the other. I'm useless in a fight, he thought, and I did that to them?

There was the BRRP-BRRP of a cop siren suddenly, frighteningly-close, and Ben immediately opened up his fists to spread palms, sighing to himself. "Fuck."

8

"You can't go in there."

Lin fit in here far too well, Ben thought as he walked towards Kalli's office, seeing her sitting at the reception desk, scrolling through her phone. "This your new gig?"

"Nah, Emmanuel stepped away, covering for a minute. I'm going out later with Dana and Pedro to pick someone up once he's done in the bathroom," she said, continuing to ignore him as the office door opened and Kalli stuck her head out. "Thanks for getting that shit off my back, by the by. Emmanuel step away?" she then directed at Lin, who nodded without looking up. "Go find Dana and Pedro and get outta here." Kalli stepped out and closed the door behind her, walking and motioning for Ben to follow. "So, how's the file room?"

Ben's little B&E at the office and the possession of the snap-out baton hadn't gone over well even though the two, cousins who claimed they'd been doing a prank and it go out of hand as a favor for their boss confessed, and he'd technically been fired. Lin more or less took his job and Ben was, through the loading entrance from now on, brought back into the firm as a "temp" in the file room a month later. "Not bad, at least the wifi reached down there." She slid a file into his hands and didn't say anything else as she stopped to talk to someone else at a cubicle, looking at the younger man like the conversation was already over. Ben walked away, opening up the case she'd "assigned" to him, under the understanding that if no one said he was on a thing he might have "accidentally" picked up, then no one could be held accountable if he went and did something about it.

At least until things blew over.

The laptop to the other network connection had been full of unwiped stuff because everyone else had assumed someone had grabbed it, or they'd forgotten it even existed in the months leading up to the company "sale" to itself to fool bankruptcy lawyers.

Hundreds of saved logins and passwords to social media accounts all promising returns on investments, and even a rough file dump full of bank info and passwords for something cryptic currency- or cryptocurrency-, Ben couldn't remember what it'd been called, related. "One big circle jerk right into each other's dicks," Pedro had called it when he'd come to bail Ben out of not-quite holding, sitting there for a day handcuffed to the bench with a ham sandwich and a bottle of water.

It turned out Kalli had been paranoid about the case, about that kind of money and that sort of shadiness involving computers and phones, and according to a few people, had laughed loudly at the letter physically mailed to her with Ben's idea. And once the laptop he'd found in that office and the two interns' confessions found their way to the client, the desire for the computers and Hector and anything else had just evaporated into the wind like a fart everyone had wanted to forget about.

Literally nothing had really changed though, otherwise. No news about any major scandals, not even, according to Lin, "on the tech blogs. She and Kalli, who had taken a liking to the ambitious woman, sat in a conference room with Ben after he had been brought back and technically speaking, the news was good, if the kind of good that indicated a return to a status quo that did nothing of value. Still, could be worse, honestly. Hector was gone, though Kalli said Pedro, who could always find anyone, had a line on him somewhere and he was safe, the new company that'd been Hector's old company that had bought itself wasn't there anymore but someone had bailed those two guys out, and they'd disappeared too, probably back to the rich parents or girlfriends who could take them on surprise vacations despite court orders.

Kalli had offered to pay for his broken window. He didn't take it though, and had left the hole in the glass open for a day before he put a piece of plywood over it to keep the pigeons out. It'd be something to hold over her head later when I need it, Ben thought.

"Bailout"

———————

"NAME?"

"Huh?"

"Name, genius. Full, please."

"Oh, uhh, sorry. Kim, Frederick Kim."

"And you're attempting to post bail for one, uhhh, hold on," Ben Miles put the forms aside on his desk, rooting through the growing stack of paper on the chair next to his desk in his loft home office. BEN MILES PRIVATE INVEST. & BAIL BONDS on the business card thumb-tacked to the apartment's front door. "Posting bail for one Kim, Michael?" Ben looked at the nervous young man sitting across from him, his foot tapping, fingers nervously playing on his knee. "Brother?"

"What? No! No, he's my cousin. Sister's husband's cousin, actually, but know how it is..."

"Yeah, I know." The Koreans in Queens were large and relatively insular extended families in Ben's experience, rivaled only by the Greeks and Italians in terms of how keep you could follow a family connection. "These are some serious charges, you know. I'm a little surprised that you're coming to me. You know I do ten percent of his bond, right? Ten percent of fifteen thousand is one thousand, five hundred dollars. Doesn't need to be up front, but I do nothing until you pony up the cash to get him out." Michael Kim,

Thirty-two, unemployed but along with an unidentified male, had been involved in a road rage incident on Queens Boulevard earlier that week when his brand-new Cadillac SUV cut off a cab that Kim claims scratched the new paint. The unidentified man took off and was at large as a witness in the case, but Kim beat the cab driver into unconsciousness with a crowbar he'd wrestled away from the older man who'd kept it under the driver's seat of his yellow cab.

Ben sighed, putting down the paperwork and staring at the nervous man, wringing his baseball cap in his hands. "Fred? Can I call you Fred? I want you to be honest with me. Why're you bailing your cousin out? Because looking at his record he's totally pulled this shit before." Ben got up from the desk, went to the fridge, and rooted through it loudly, clanking and banging around as Frederick Kim shifted nervously in his chair, turning around to watch ben like a nervous dog trying to keep the threatening man in his sights at all times. Standing up with an armful of canned beer and a box of pizza, the let the door of the fridge close on its own, coming back to the desk. "Here, have a drink. You hungry?" He flipped the pizza box open as he passed a beer to Kim, opening his and grabbing a slice of the cold pepperoni pizza, stuffing it into his mouth. If anything, I'm surprised you came to me at all. You feel bad about fleeing the accident before your cousin beat the shit outta that cabbie?"

"What?" Kim said loudly, almost jumping out of the seat and spilling the open can of beer he was staring at and nursing. "No! that wasn't me, I wasn't there? Wh-what are you talking about?"

"Come on man, don't lie to me, I know that's why, otherwise your family'd probably cut him off for something as stupid as this." The last time Ben dealt with a Korean family bailing out an addict family member in Brooklyn he could barely get any of the on the phone before Kalli Kiliaris, his far-more successful bondswoman, former-but-sometimes-current-boss, PI, and friend, reminded him that they probably had been pressured into putting up bail by the younger family members, since the parents had refused to address the issue at all of an addict shaming the family name and embarrassing them in their neighborhood and church congregation.

"No, I wasn't there! I was at home with my mom when he..."

"When he what?" How did you know he did it?" Ben was leaning forward now, quiet but intense, grilling the other man who was clearly feeling nervous and trapped in the office-cum-apartment in the chair in front of the big battered old office desk Ben used for everything.

"H-he's not right sometimes, you know?" He was less nervous now as the focus moved away from him, giving Frederick a chance to paint Michael Kim as the aggressor, trying to convince Ben. "You know, he gets mad, he does stupid shi-I mean, stuff," Frederick finally settling into the chair and eyeing Ben, reaching for a slice of pizza. "Please, go ahead man," the bondsman said, sitting back at the desk and putting his feet up.

"So he's got an anger problem?" Ben said, laughing a bit. "Oh yeah, the other man continued, clearly enjoying the chance to further help build the case against his cousin. "When we were kids, his parents don't like to ever mention it but he almost got kicked out of high school? For a fight, someone got mad at him and he beat the crap out of them." Michael Kim was six-two, two hundred pounds of muscle and had been, from everyone else Ben had talked to, that size most of his life, a big mean bully of the highest order.

Ben wasn't surprised to hear that, but was still curious. "So what, you think that the cabbie just cut him off and he chased him down to fuck him up or something?"

"Yeah I guess," Frederick was suddenly quiet, looking down at the beer and pizza in his hands, and again unable to meet Ben's gaze. "He's...well I know that his parents won't ever see it because they're older and he fools them, and mine don't want to admit it, but he's pretty fucked up."

"That so?" Ben mused, standing up and going over to one of the boxes scattered atop the nearest file cabinet, already overflowing with paper scraps and carbon copies and printouts, rifling through it. "So I guess he's a shitty driver too, with that tank of a Caddy he was in, barreling down the road."

"Yeah," Frederick said quietly, "really, I don't know how he has his license."

"He doesn't," Ben said simply, cleaning up the food and beer cans, walking around Frederick to the fridge and trash. "I checked, earlier when you called me before you came over. DMV says your cousin's got no license, but the guy at the dealership says he paid in cash and had someone with him to drive it who had a license. You know that it's not illegal to buy a car if you don't have a license in the state of New York?"

"Y-you what?"

"Well, I didn't go to the dealership or call them, I called a friend of mine who did it for me. She's much better at conning second-rate Caddy dealers into remembering stuff that they'd normally never tell the cops or me." Ben sat down at the desk and thumbed through his phone, reading off something, nodding. "Yeah, he said your cousin showed up and put own a lot of cash and was with a nervous-looking skinny guy. His words, not mine." Frederick was getting noticeably agitated again now, looking up and down and around and back down at his wringing hands. "You, right?"

"No! I'm telling you it wasn't me!"

"So if I take a picture of you," Ben said as the phone's camera clicked its artificial shutter-click sound, "and then I show it to the car dealership guy and have that talk to your cousin's lawyer, they're not gonna hear him say that you drove off in the car with your cousin in the passenger seat after you bought it that day?"

Frederick jumped up from the chair, running to the front door. "G-g-get the fuck away from me!" he screamed, fumbling with the doorknob as Ben took off after him, barely getting a handful of sweatshirt before the other man slipped through the door and down the building's stairwell fast, taking the steps two at a time. "Goddammit," the bondsman muttered, taking off after him.

Ben took the stairs as fast as he could after the other man who was doing them two at a time, knowing that the stairs were full of gaps and creaky spot that were throwing Frederick off as he tried to flee and that let Ben know he had a chance to catch up. Pre-war and barely-maintained, Ben tripped and feel regularly on them, and he was pretty sure potential clients stayed away when the oft-broken elevator was presented to them on the first floor and the hand-painted NO WORK sign was taped to the buttons.

The front door of the building slammed as he turned the last corner down the stairwell, and Ben started muttering under his breath as he pulled the heavy door open, bolting down the block to follow the string of knocked-over pedestrians, a few pointing and the rest staggering in confusion as the PI worked his way through the crowd as fast as he could. "Jesus wept Fred!" he yelled, hoping the other man would hear him as the crowd started to thin out on the sidewalk and the neighborhood was slowly changing, the former warehouse district of Queens reverting back into actually being a warehouse district, the crowds now consisting of a few delivery men and door managers for the various businesses they passed. The sounds of the highway, running parallel with the neighborhood, were slowly getting louder and he could see Frederick down the block. "Goddamnit" he repeated under his breath, ignoring the burning in his lungs as he worked to try to keep up. The other man was younger and faster, but he was burning up more, already slowing down. Ben was slower, but persistent, and being able to follow Frederick down the street, around corners and under the overheads of the highway.

He was gaining.

"Frederick's cousin and a witness had already identified him, but he' been hard to nail down, a busy worker and student who somehow seemed to avoid the police without even trying, making the whole thing even harder until Ben and his ex-boss and friend, PI and bondswoman Kalli Kiliaris worked out a way to get him in, Kalli convincing his parents to help out to save the favored prodigal son in jail for what the nervous jumpy cousin did, ditching him at the scene of an accident to take the blame and letting a serious criminal past doom him, all so Frederick could save his legal career and make his own parents proud.

"Seriously Fred! Come on, slow down!" Ben yelled, knowing that he was close enough to be heard, and then the other man stumbled. A crack in the sidewalk forced up a fraction of an inch. A fraction of an inch, and the fragment caught the tip of his sneaker and Frederick went flying down the sidewalk, a "whump" flying out of his lungs as the form landed, skidding down and over in the bizarre pattern towards the curb and the slick black tarmac-dirty street next to a parked van.

Ben slowed down, almost tripping over his own feet as he tried to stop and not fall over the downed man. He knelt down, sitting on Frederick and crossing his arms across his chest, "Jesus wept kid," he gasped, trying to catch his breath in jagged and full rough rasps, "You are fast."

Afterword

Working on this has been weird, mostly because it's involved going back through older work, and it's a thing that I usually don't do. Honestly though?

I mean, it's not that bad.

There are some bits where I can definitely see the work of a somewhat-younger brain, and the times I've tried before to look at my older work in general makes me realize just how much I've had to really think about how the words that I put down not only tell a story but set a tone and attitude that I don't necessarily want to set anymore, because I can recognize how that tone and attitude are not that healthy to indulge in. Not to say that I've learned to self-censor, but rather to recognize just how to make a good story work without having to rely on cheap hacks of storytelling and language that honestly, just fuckin' cheapen storytelling and writing overall.

I'm glad I did this. I'm glad I can do this, of going over old work and unpublished work that should have been finished before or...if we're being honest, never seen the light of day but I used it like an exercise to just get something out of my head.

Ben Miles was both my "baby" but also my learning experience for writing the kind of fiction I finally really wanted to, that reflected the language of my influences, the style of my interactions, and the way I viewed the world around me. He's totally me, if I was far bolder and far less smart, or maybe smarter, I guess. And like me, he's always learning and hoping to just not get his ass kicked. If that's all anyone gets out of this, then that's what mattered here.

Thanks for reading. Will Ben Miles ever be back? Who knows, honestly.

ABOUT THE AUTHOR

Costa Koutsoutis is a writer and college professor from New York City. He's written fiction and nonfiction for a variety of outlets, has worked as a doorman for punk shows, loves to cook, and is aware that yes, he is a grouch. You can find out more about him and his work at costak.wordpress.com.

Also by Costa Koutsoutis

Running The Train And All The Stories: The Complete Ben Miles
Collection
Lightning Crashes Here: Essays
The Go-Between
Stronger Than Swords: A Collection of Fantasy & Science Fiction
Short Stories
The Vast Cold Dark

Watch for more at costak.wordpress.com.